HIGHLAND *Raven*

MELANIE KARSAK

Published by Clockpunk Press
PO Box 560367
Rockledge, FL 32956-0367
http://www.clockpunkpress.com

Editing by Cat Carlson Amick
Proofreading by Becky Stephens Editing
Cover art by Liliana Sanches
Formatting by Inkstain Interior Book Designing

OTHER WORKS BY MELANIE KARSAK

THE AIRSHIP RACING CHRONICLES
Chasing the Star Garden
Chasing the Green Fairy

THE HARVESTING SERIES
The Harvesting
Midway
The Shadow Aspect

THE CELTIC BLOOD SERIES
Highland Raven

—for Mother

prologue

I'VE BEEN DEFAMED. THE BARD of *Avon dubbed me a villainess, an angry, evil murderess. I'm forever painted as an ambitious, blood-hungry queen. They'd have you take me for a mad woman. Slander. Small men tell lies. Poets tell half-truths. Maybe I am a bit mad, but who wouldn't be after all I have seen? Regardless, I don't want you to believe such deceits. I don't want my name to go down in the annuals of times with such epitaphs. My name. What is my name? Have you ever heard it? Did your professor of English ever utter it? My name is quite the mystery. My father gave me one, my aunt dubbed me with another, but in the end, my wyrdness ruled all.*

I was born in the year 1010 of an Irish princess and an heir to the throne of Scotland. My mother was the reward from a raid into Ireland and a false treaty thereafter. She's forgotten now, but I want you to know her name. I owe her that. They called her Emer after the Irish legend of Cu Chulainn. She was tall, thin, and had blonde hair that stretched to the floor. My mother died a short nine months after marrying my father, whose name was Boite. My beginning brought her end. They believe she lived sixteen years. Not a long life. And me, I came into the world killing.

My ill-fated birth came at the end of another of my father's campaigns. As the corpses were paraded past the castle to the burial mound, I emerged squalling from the womb. I was handed to my father who was covered in more blood than me; the sticky red liquid on his chainmail stained the white of my swaddles.

"See here, child," my father whispered, lifting me to the open window casement. "These men are of your blood. I set the mark of the old gods upon you," he said, tracing ancient runes upon my brow, my natal blood mixing with the blood of the dead men. "Avenge your kinsman. I call upon the Morrigu, the ancient and dead Goddess of these lands, and ask her to claim you. Let her rise up and take you. Let her whisper battle cries for lullabies. Avenge with the magic of the old gods. Rise up, child, and carry our banner forth. Remember that you are a child of Kenneth MacAlpin's line and bring vengeance."

Dark clouds moved across the sky occluding the full moon. A raven's shrill pierced the silence. The old gods had listened.

"Hear now, sweet babe, Gruoch, hear how the raven calls."

Thus the first name fell upon me, Gruoch, an awful sounding name uttered from an angry and vengeful man. Behind my father, the midwives crossed themselves. Though he attended the mass of the White Christ, those close to my father knew his heart belonged to the old ones. And me, the farthest from him, felt his beliefs most of all. Perhaps, in this, he did me a single justice.

One

"TOIL AND TROUBLE," MY AUNT Madelaine grumbled playfully as she shook me awake. "Raising you has been nothing but toil and trouble. Wake up, Little Corbie."

Little Corbie. All my life she had called me Little Corbie, her little raven, on account of my looks: raven-black hair, pale skin, and lavender-colored eyes. I yawned tiredly and rolled over, pulling my covers over my head. I was too sleepy to get into mischief, but Madelaine's voice told me she was ripe with it.

"Lazy," she scolded, shaking my shoulder. "Get up. We're waiting for you."

Through my sleep-clouded eyes, I peered out from my blankets past the waterfall of Madelaine's curly red hair to see the silhouette of Tavis, my aunt's brawny champion, in the doorway. Madelaine's husband, Alister, was still away, and she wasn't going to let even a moment of her temporary freedom pass unenjoyed.

3

"The night is still fighting the morning and so am I," I complained sleepily, but my hazy head started to clear, and the first glimmer of nervous excitement filled my stomach. Madelaine's waywardness almost always resulted in fun.

"The raven caws," Tavis said from the door. "I'll meet my ladies in the stable." The door clapped shut behind him, and I heard the sound of his footsteps recede down the stone castle hallway. I looked out the window. The night's sky was fading into hazy gray as the first hint of rosy pink illuminated the skyline.

Madelaine crossed the room quickly, her fast movement becoming a blur of swirling skirts as she gathered up my riding clothes and dumped them on the end of my bed. In the heap I saw my leather riding breeches, an emerald-colored tunic, and some pale green undergarments.

With a heavy sigh, I got out of bed. "And where are we going?" I asked as I pulled on my clothes.

"Out, out! To the forest. Amongst the trees. Somewhere where we can run wild," Madelaine said with a laugh as she tossed me my riding cloak. "I can smell the sap running, can't you? I swear I could smell daffodils on the wind this morning," Madelaine said in a singsong.

I couldn't help but smile. Madelaine was my father Boite's half-sister, and I adored her. "Can't the forest come to us?" I asked with a laugh.

"Don't worry. The morning air will perk you up," she said with a grin. Once I was dressed, she grabbed my hand, and we headed downstairs. The castle was quiet. Only a few servants were stirring as we wound

4

down the stairwell, passing through the great hall. A fire roared in the grand fireplace. It burned off the cool morning air.

Moving quickly and quietly, we headed toward the stables. The morning sky was lit up with rose, orange, and violet light. Thin strips of clouds streaked the horizon. As we crossed the yard, we stirred up the flock of chickens that had just risen for their morning meal.

Aggie, the servant girl, was just about to feed them.

"My Ladies," Aggie said with a smile. A tender girl with reddish-blonde hair and face full of freckles, she was always trying to help me improve embroidery. Despite her best efforts, I left every lesson with bloody fingertips.

"Aggie, sweet girl, tell your mother I'll be back by supper!" Madelaine called, referring to Ally, the head of Madelaine's domestics.

"Of course, My Lady," Aggie said with a grin. She winked playfully at me.

I grinned, rolled my eyes knowingly, and waved good-bye to her.

Madelaine's capricious ways were well-known by the servants, but they never betrayed her trust. After all, everyone knew how vicious Alister, Madelaine's husband, truly was. Everyone loved and pitied her, me included. And when it came to her household, Madelaine was always first to defend and protect them, though there was little she could say in anyone's defense when Alister found a reason to hate…or punish…or want. I shuddered. I'd learned the hard way that it was dangerous to be close to him. I swallowed hard and tried not to think about it. Alister was gone, for now, and Madelaine was right. You could smell spring in the air.

The yard was a muddy mess. It rained nonstop for three days. All of the grass outside the walls of the tall stone citadel had been worn down to the bare earth. While the rains had finally relented, my boots were caked with mud by the time we reached the stables. Tavis was waiting outside the barn with our horses already saddled.

"Lady Raven," he said and smiled as he held out his hand, helping me onto my beloved black horse, Kelpie. The steed was the last gift my father had ever given me. Given his bewitching color—midnight-black without a speck of disruption save his dark-brown eyes—I named him for the shape-shifting horse spirits said to haunt the lochs.

"What mischief have you been up to, my water horse?" I whispered once I mounted, leaning over to hug his neck and whisper in his ear. I inhaled his sweet, hay-frosted scent. The horse flicked his ears backward to listen to me then nickered softly. I patted his neck.

Tavis helped Madelaine mount her chestnut-colored palfrey then swung up onto his own steed.

Madeline smiled at me, the first rays of morning light making her red hair glow like flames. "Ready?" she asked, her green eyes twinkling.

I nodded.

With a click of the tongue, she spurred her horse away from the castle. Laughing, Tavis reined his horse in after her.

"Come on, Corbie," Tavis called as we rode toward a forest trail. "And don't fall asleep in the saddle."

The air was cool and fresh. Once the sun had risen, it warmed my raven-black tresses. Despite my best effort to keep up with Madelaine's energy, my head bobbed drowsily. She and Tavis meandered down the forest path, flirting shamelessly. Madelaine's red hair shone bright as a cardinal amongst the trees, her gown, the color of brilliant blue forget-me-nots, hugged her perfect shape.

After half a morning's ride, we came to a lush green valley between three high mountains where a small, still loch reflected the periwinkle-blue sky. Large white clouds were reflected on the smooth surface of the water.

"Let's stop here," Madelaine called when we neared a small clutch of apple trees. She smiled brightly. Such trips outside the castle were a rare treat. Only when Alister was away could Madelaine roam the countryside, always with Tavis at her side, enjoying her freedom. She was, after all, a wild thing. She moped like a caged bird in the castle, but the forest—and Tavis—brought her back to life. Since I was almost always part of her capricious plans, I enjoyed the change as much as she did, though I hated to wake up so early.

Tavis helped Madelaine and I dismount then spread out a blanket while Madelaine pulled a wine jug and goblets from her bag. I took off Kelpie's bridle to let him wander where he pleased. He went to the loch and drank deeply from the fresh spring water.

Madelaine filled three goblets and handed one to each of us. "To this fine spring day," she toasted.

"And to my ladies," Tavis added, tapping his goblet against Madelaine's and mine.

He drank his wine in large gulps, Madelaine refilling his glass when it was empty. She then corked the wine and lay back under the trees. A small wind shook the pink and white apple blossoms, showering her in petals. She giggled when the pearly wisps of silk landed on her face, but she didn't open her eyes. Tavis laughed and gently blew the petals off. The sweet scent of the blossoms filled the air.

"It's getting warm. I can smell the earth coming to life again," Tavis said.

"Humm," Madelaine commented as she stretched out, seeming to doze under the warm sun. She was settling in just as I was starting to finally feel awake. From the way Tavis was looking at Madelaine, I had an inkling they wouldn't mind some privacy, so I decided to wander.

"I'll be back in a bit," I said, standing.

"Leaving already?" Madelaine asked teasingly. Her eyes still closed, she didn't see me roll my eyes at her.

Tavis rose and went to his horse, returning with a sword. "My spare," he said as he belted the scabbard around my waist. His hands were deft, and as he leaned in close to me, I smelled the heavy scent of lavender oil on him. I breathed in deeply. My heart beat a little faster. "Yell if trouble finds you."

"No trouble will find her," Madelaine commented sleepily.

I raised an eyebrow at her but said nothing.

I STEPPED LIGHTLY AROUND THE lake. Salamanders and fish swam in the clear water amongst the high cattails.

A soft breeze chased the winter chill away, filling the air with the smell of damp earth. Above me, a raven shrilled and flew into the valley. I followed it.

The raven flew from tree to tree into a very old forest. Here the trees were massive, the old oaks reaching far overhead. The bird hopped from one branch to another, leading me around a bog where bright-colored dragonflies zipped from place to place. It cawed at me then led me deeper into the woods. All the hair on the back of my neck had risen. Ravens were the emblem of my family. Surely the bird was a harbinger. I followed the inky bird to a stream where it roosted in a tall willow at the water's edge. Cawing down once more at me, it then took off quickly, disappearing into the sky. My nerves were set on edge. I looked all around, expecting…something. But there was nothing. I sighed. I was in the middle of the forest near a fallen tree at the edge of a stream with only the eyes of the woods on me. I had followed the raven where? To the middle of nowhere. It was peaceful and far from the confines of castle life, but something told me Madelaine was having a much more exciting time than me.

Sighing again, I spotted a small clutch of snowdrops grew near a fallen tree. I picked a handful and relaxed into a niche amongst the branches and started weaving a crown. I breathed in deeply. I loved the loamy smell of the earth and the sound of the babbling brook.

Intent on my task, I hardly noticed the passage of time. An hour must have passed when I was suddenly struck with a strange feeling. I felt someone near me. I looked up to find a woman standing on the other side of the creek, just twelve feet away, watching me. Fear washed over me; I bit my lip.

My hands trembling, I set the flower wreath on my lap and studied her. Was she friend or foe? Over one shoulder she had slung a game bag. An herb pouch hung from her belt, and she held a bow in her hand. She had long brown hair pulled into a braid. She wore the leather jerkin of a man and pants to match. On her hands she wore rough leather gloves, and the hilt of a dagger stuck out from the top of her boot.

"You are Gruoch," she said calmly, her voice deep and raspy.

I didn't reply.

"Gruoch, tell Madelaine the Goddess calls. Tell her to bring you at the full moon."

My heart thundered in my chest. Gruoch. No one called me by that name except my father. When he had visited in my twelfth year, he and Madelaine talked in hushed tones deep into the night. Curious, I spied on them through a crack in the door.

"The Goddess will call her when the time is right. We will have to give her up then," my father had said in his deep, gruff voice. I could just see him through a gap in the closed feasting hall door. A tall fire roared, casting orange light on them as they sat at the slat-wood table. His long black hair was pulled away from his face by two braids which were tied at the back with a silver raven knot pendant. His hair shimmered blue in the firelight. My father was a hulking creature, but as he leaned in toward Madelaine, who looked as thin as a goldenrod beside him, his rugged features were gentle. He tenderly took her hand.

"It will be hard to let her go," Madelaine replied, and I saw her wipe a tear from her cheek.

My father kissed her on the forehead. "I am so grateful that you've loved her like she was your own. I could not…"

Madelaine shook her head and entwined her fingers in his, comforting him. "It was not in your hand."

"But I love her so," he whispered. "As much as I can. I hope she knows."

"Even if she doesn't understand now, one day she will. After all, we have the same blood in our veins. Our line must serve."

"Yes…we all answer our call," he said, touching an all-too-apparent bruise on Madelaine's cheek. Such bruises were the ongoing handiwork of her husband, Alister. "No matter your will. No matter the price."

Moving his hand away from his bruise, she replied, "We all endure. But where you can, use better sense than your father."

Madelaine and my father were half-siblings; they shared the same mother. When Madelaine's father had died, her mother had been wed to Kenneth, my grandfather. Their marriage produced two noble sons, Boite (my father), and King Malcolm (Boite's elder brother), and so by marriage Madelaine became their sister and at the mercy of Kenneth's decisions. It was he who had wed her to Alister in political alliance.

"Wed her to a kind man or don't wed her at all," Madelaine pleaded to Boite.

"May the Goddess let it be so," my father whispered.

"May the Goddess let it be so," Madelaine chimed solemnly.

That winter, in an effort to pacify strained relations with the English, King Malcolm sent my father and a small army to Wales to help English King Cnut settle an uprising. Heavily outnumbered, with reinforcements far behind, my father died. I once heard Alister say that Malcolm had sent my father to his death, eliminating my father's threat to his throne. Maybe he was right. But at the time, the line of succession didn't matter much to me. I mourned the death of my father.

As I sat looking at the woman standing across from me, I wondered about their words. Was this what Madelaine and my father had meant? Was this my call? This moment? Fear and excitement gripped my throat, strangling the words and questions that wanted to come out. I rose and took a step toward the creek, toward the stranger.

The woman smiled, her lips pulling to one side in a bemused look, and turned from the creek. "See you soon, Little Raven," she called as she made her way back into the woods, disappearing amongst the trees. I took a deep breath, and with weak knees, turned to make my way back to Madelaine.

two

BY THE TIME I RETURNED to the loch, the sun was high in the sky. I walked toward the trees where I had last seen my aunt, but I was distracted. My mind thundered over my encounter in the woods. Who was that woman? What did it mean that the Goddess had called? Busy with my own thoughts, I was surprised when I finally looked up and saw Madelaine lying naked under the trees with Tavis. I could hear their light moans as he moved himself over her.

Startled and feeling a bit stupid, I sat down at the water's edge away from them, hidden by the high cattails. I felt my cheeks redden, but my curiosity got the better of me. Peering through the leaves, I gazed toward the intermeshed figures of my aunt and her lover. Their hands roved in hungry caresses over one another's bodies. My aunt was beautiful, her red hair lying like a pallet around her. I felt ashamed of my curiosity, but the thought of being with a man excited me. At the age of sixteen, I was still a virgin, but I could be called for a marriage contract at any time. I loved the idea of being in love. I wanted to be wanted. And I hoped I ended up with someone like Tavis. He was kind and funny, and his body was glorious. His muscular back and round ass glimmered in the sunlight, enhancing his every curve.

Tavis kissed Madelaine passionately then lay his head on her chest. She stroked his golden hair, and I could just catch the murmur of their whispers on the wind. A moment later, Tavis rose carefully, tickled Madelaine's chin, and ran naked to the loch. He disappeared under the water as my aunt began to redress. Eager to tell Madelaine what had happened, I rose and walked toward her. It occurred to me as I walked, however, that maybe Madelaine already knew. Maybe she'd planned it, or at least suspected, all along. I hid my eagerness in order to find out.

She spotted me as I rounded the loch and smiled widely at me.

Grinning, Tavis waved from the loch. I poured myself a glass of wine, sipping the red liquid as Madelaine and I watched Tavis swim toward the shore. He rose from the water and walked toward us, his naked body dripping wet. I looked at him without modesty. In the end, he blushed and began to redress.

"So where did you go?" Madelaine asked.

"Into the forest."

Madelaine nodded. "See anything interesting?"

"Well, nothing as interesting as you did," I said with a wink, making Madelaine giggle unapologetically. "But I did make this for you," I said, handing her the flower wreath.

"Thank you," she said, putting the ring on her head.

"Oh, yes, and I followed a raven into an old forest. A woman there told me that you are to bring me at the next full moon," I added offhand.

Madelaine's cheerful gaze turned serious. She took my hand and looked at me closely. "Who said this to you?"

"The huntress," I replied, gazing into my aunt's green eyes. To my surprise, they'd become watery.

"The huntress," my aunt repeated.

I nodded. "I was near the stream by the tall oaks. A woman with long brown hair came to me there."

Madelaine nodded and smiled softly. "Her name is Uald."

"And I'm to go at the next full moon? Where?"

"The Goddess calls," Madelaine replied and pulled me into a deep hug, squeezing me tightly.

I RODE AHEAD OF MADELAINE and Tavis on the way back to the castle. The full moon was only three eves away. I felt overwhelmed with questions. Where was it that I was supposed to go? For how long? And why had my father planned this fate for me?

A mess of nerves, I asked to take my dinner in my room that evening; I wanted to be alone with my thoughts. Perching carefully on the windowsill, I looked out at the grounds around the castle. The landscape sparkled silver in the moonlight. The moon was a nearly-full silver orb. I snubbed out my candles, letting my chamber fill with silver light. The moonbeams made my pale flesh glow. It was late when Madelaine finally entered.

She sighed heavily and sat down on the side of my bed. "I will tell Alister you are being sent to a convent until a suitable marriage match is made for you, that you will learn the ways of the White Christ and to read and write Latin. I will tell him that this was your father's wish." She paused then, looking off into the distance. "The convent...well, it is a lie he will believe." She turned to me. "My Little Corbie, your father wanted this for you. It has all been arranged for a long time. You will go to learn the ways of our family. It was your father's true wish. Boite would not have his daughter turn to the White Christ, to deny the old gods. You must learn the ancient arts. Old magic flows through the beating heart of this realm. It is your duty to know these ancient truths. It is part of who we are."

Neither Madelaine nor I ever partook in the ways of the White Christ. As a Lord should, Alister kept priests in the castle, in particular, the annoying Father Edwin who always dogged his shadow. I avoided him at all costs. He was a vile man. On more than one occasion, Father Edwin had tried to *correct* my pagan ways.

Two years before, on a lonely winter's night, a bard had sung the legend of Tristan and Isolde after dinner. In the ballad, the young lovers were torn apart by a marriage contract which ordered Isolde to marry Tristan's uncle Mark. The miserable Isolde, married off to Mark of Cornwall, had tried to catch a glimpse of her lover by scrying in the flames. Through the eyes of the fire, the fair Isolde saw that Tristan had married another. It nearly broke the poor maiden's heart.

I became enamored with the idea of seeing images in the fire. That night, after everyone had gone to bed, I'd tried to catch a glimpse of my father through the feasting hall fire. I was staring into the fire, trying to work magic like I'd heard in the story, when I'd felt someone come up behind me.

"What are you doing?" a voice asked.

I had been sitting there a long time. Maybe I'd been staring too closely into the flames: I felt dizzy. The heat of the fire had made me sweat. I never saw my father in the flames, but I'd seen what looked like a snowy white field dotted with ravens.

"I'm looking for my father," I replied weakly.

A moment later, I felt the sharp sting of someone's hand on my cheek. I looked up to find Father Edwin standing over me.

"Devilry," he swore, his whole body shaking. "You are conjuring the devil in your uncle's very hall! Would you bring Satan into this place?" His thin body leaned threateningly over me. He shouted with such venom that his spit splashed on my cheek. Shocked, I shuddered as I stared at the priest's pock-marked face.

When I didn't answer him, he lifted his hand as if he would hit me once more.

"Enough," a voice called from the doorway. I turned to find Alister standing there. His long brown hair hung in a greasy tumble. His stomach had grown so large over the course of the winter that the bottom of his bloated belly peaked out from under his tunic. He was lighting a pipe, the red of the flame making a collage of shadows and red hues across his face. "Enough, Edwin.

I'll school her," Alister told the priest as he crossed the hall. He staggered as he walked.

"Yes, My Lord," the priest said, glaring at me once more, and then smiling before he left me and my uncle alone.

"Little Raven. Come," Alister called. He dragged a chair before the fire, the legs screeching across the stone floor. He set the pipe down and beckoned for me to sit on his lap. He reeked of ale and the heavy scent of angelica root smoke from the pipe.

Still feeling dizzy from looking into the flames, and my cheek smarting with pain, I did as I was told. But my instincts were on alarm. I knew well that Alister was not to be trusted.

"Does it hurt?" Alister asked, touching my cheek lightly.

The stink of body odor emanated from him. His hair held the light scent of ox fat. Alister stroked my cheek with his sweaty hand then rubbed his fingers up and down the length of my neck.

"Yes," I replied quietly, forcing my stomach not to revolt. My intuition told me to run away.

"Poor thing. I won't let him touch you ever again. Don't worry. But tell me, did you see anything in the flames?" Alister asked as his hand softly caressed my shoulder.

I shook my head.

"Come now, Little Corbie, I know your blood is full of the old magic. Tell your foster father what you saw."

His hand rubbed my arm, his thumb pressing against my breast over and over again.

"I saw ravens…ravens in the snow."

"Ravens in the snow?" he asked, his hand now rubbing my leg. "Poor girl. How frightening. Here," he said, pulling me against him. This time, he moved my bottom over his pelvis, and I felt his hard cock pressing into me. His hands caught the hem of my dress, his sticky fingers sliding up the insides of my bare legs, my thighs. I gasped. I'd seen Alister use the same move more than a dozen times on the serving girls. I knew what came next. I just couldn't believe he'd try it on me.

I tried to pull away, but he grabbed me roughly, squeezing my inner thighs, forcing my legs open. He tore my undergarments aside; I felt the fabric rip as I struggled to be free. But he was stronger than me. Forcing my legs open, he jabbed his fingers inside me.

"Don't move, Little Raven," he whispered in my ear. I struggled, feeling sick as his fingers jabbed into me. "You'll like fucking as much as your sweet auntie does. We can keep each other warm all winter."

The door to the feasting hall opened.

"Corbie?" Madelaine called. I saw the look on her face as she took in the scene. Her pretty features contorted into a weird grimace.

Alister let me go.

Gagging, I fell to the floor.

Madelaine rushed across the room, bending to pick me up. Tears were already rushing down my cheeks. My stomach tossed.

"Go upstairs," Madelaine whispered to me, but I was frozen in place, staring, horrified, at Alister.

"Christ, Madelaine, you're such a nuisance. Barren cunt. What good are you, anyway?" Alister asked sarcastically as he rose. Stepping toward us, he punched Madelaine in the gut.

Gasping, Madelaine fell to her knees.

"Whore. You're nothing but a whore," he said. Grabbing Madelaine by the hair, he lifted her to her feet and slammed her against the wall. I heard her moan when she hit the hard stones. He was advancing on her again when I noticed that a carving knife lying forgotten on the table. Jumping to my feet, I grabbed the knife and put myself between Alister and Madelaine.

"Don't touch her," I said, lifting the knife menacingly.

"Well now, what do we have here?" Alister asked with a laugh, but he didn't come closer.

"Keep your filthy hands off both of us, or next time I'll chop your fingers off," I spat. I hoped Alister wouldn't notice my hands trembling. I clutched the knife handle so hard my hand hurt.

"Well, there it is...now that is the blood of a true MacAlpin, not some half-blooded bitch from Strathclyde like you," Alister said to Madelaine then turned to me. "You've got your daddy's blood, girl," Alister said laughing. He picked up his pipe and lit it, the heavy smoke twisting upward and turned and left the room, banging the wooden door shut behind him.

I dropped the knife. It hit the stone floor with a clatter. I turned to my Madelaine. "Are you all right?"

She collapsed into my arms. "I'm so sorry," she heaved, grabbing me tightly. Her whole body was shaking. "Did he...did he ruin you?"

I shook my head.

"May the Great Mother watch over us both. He's drunk tonight. He's lost even to his worst self. He knows

20

better. King Malcolm would execute him. I'm so sorry," she whispered.

My stomach rolled. I could still feel the sharp prick of his fingers in me, crooked, sharp and vile. I felt sick and angry. I felt polluted. And even as bad as it was for me, my heart ached for Madelaine. I knew that what I saw was just a hint of what happened between them behind closed doors. Madelaine had faced far worse, worse than she would ever name. Her body, all the bruises, told the tales she never spoke. In Alister's house, no one was safe.

I squeezed my eyes tight, forcing the memory of that night away, and tried to focus on Madelaine who was still speaking of what it meant that the Goddess had called: "You will go amongst our wise women," Madelaine was saying. "They are women of the old ways. They will teach you our faith, the ways of our people. You have no need to fear," Madelaine explained.

"I'm not afraid," I whispered. At least, I was not afraid of them.

Dark clouds rolled over the moon. Everything grew black. Madelaine fell silent and did not speak again until moonlight lit the room once more. "Your soul is very old," she whispered. "Even as a babe, you were always...different. You belonged to the otherworld. I will miss you," she added and rose, leaving me to my solitude.

Three

WITH THE BLARE OF A trumpet, a courier arrived the next morning with news that Alister and his men would be home by evening. The house was set aflutter. The beds were filled with fresh straw, the stairs were scrubbed, the cattle slaughtered, and wine casks were brought up from the cellars. Madelaine, paler than the moon, moved through the house dispatching orders. Alister had been away for a month. The cooks and grooms had vacationed from their hard work. The serving girls had enjoyed empty beds.

That night, the light from Alister's men's torches glared through the dark, heralding his arrival. I watched from my window as he arrived at the castle gate and was met by Tavis whose formal position in the castle was sentinel and chief guard. Their exchange was brief and stiff.

The smell of roasting meats and wood smoke soon wafted upstairs from the feasting hall. I could hear the call for ale reverberating off the timbers and stones.

Lord Alister wanted ale, not wine. I feared for anyone who happened to get in his way, myself included. After the incident in the feasting hall, Alister's eyes never left me. He was a snake lying in wait.

I watched the activity in the yard. Some of my uncle's men rode back into the night to their awaiting families. Others pitched tents around the castle. The smell of campfire smoked filled the valley. The sweet sounds of harps and bagpipes rose up from the hall alongside rowdy cheers.

A short while later, Madelaine rapped on my door and entered. "Will you come down?" she asked, closing the door behind her as she headed to my trunk full of dresses. We both knew it was not really a question. Neither of use wanted to go to the hall, and neither of us had a choice. It was our duty to attend. Ladies of our station were expected to make any appearance. Anything less could be taken as a slight to the noble lords in attendance. And Madelaine, most of all, had to play the dutiful wife, lest she earn Alister's swift and brutal retribution. The cheerful glow on my aunt's face was gone, and her green eyes looked haunted with the look of smothered terror.

Madelaine pulled a fur-trimmed black velvet dress from my trunk. I frowned but said nothing. It would gain me nothing to complain and would only make Madelaine feel worse than she already felt.

Once I changed, we headed back to the feasting hall. Loud voices, the stench of ale, and rude talk wafted from the room. Therein, drunken revelry abounded. The room was so brightly lit that it made me squint. Madelaine squeezed my hand, but I could feel her fingers had grown cold. I hated Alister. I hated his men. I hated their ale hall. I hated the discord it brought: vomiting drunks, groping hands, and my aunt's sorrow.

"Ah, my niece," Alister called.

The men whistled and banged their ale horns against the wooden table.

Madelaine led me to the head of the table. The room was so full of smoke that it burned my eyes. I noticed that Father Edwin had returned as well. He sat near my uncle at the head of the table. He'd grown a scraggly beard while he was gone; it barely hid his pock-marked face. I shuddered.

"Corbie! Come," Alister called with a laugh. His eyes, already tinged ale-red, tried to focus on me. The smell of hops and body odor reeked from him. He'd grown fatter in the month away, his belly looking rounder than ever. And he had not changed from his mud-splatted riding clothes. I felt a lump rise into my throat. How abhorred it was to be near him. I couldn't stand the sight of him. "How is my niece?" he asked, motioning for me to sit beside him. Father Edwin looked away from me.

"Well, Uncle," I replied politely.

Madelaine turned to leave but Alister grabbed her arm and pulled her roughly back. "Where do you think you're going?"

"My Lord's kitchens need attention," she answered.

He let her go. "Then be away with you," he said, slapping her on the ass as she turned to leave. He laughed loudly as Madelaine hurried off and turned his attention to me. "Well, Little Corbie, what did you do while I was away?"

"Women's things, my uncle."

"Women's things," he repeated then laughed. "And what are women's things?"

"Sewing, gossiping, and talking about babies, of course," I replied flatly, looking forward. Alister had no imagination beyond the obvious expectations.

My uncle laughed out loud. "Indeed, women's things." He set his hand on the back of my head and stroked my hair, his hand moving down the length of my hair to the small of my back.

My stomach turned, and my body shook. I shifted away from his touch, turning to face him. His hand dropped away. "Any news from court?" I asked.

"News?" he asked with a snort. "Nothing to concern you, lass, unless you want to talk over strategies, war, or fucking!" he said then laughed out loud, the other lords around him joining his laughter. "Though," he said, leaning in toward me, his hand stroking my back again, "maybe you're finally ready to start talking about fucking," he whispered in my ear, "I still remember how sweet your perfume was," he added, then sniffed his fingers and laughed out loud, his breath reeking of meat and ale. Mortified, I turned away. I felt like someone had poured ice water over me; my flesh rose into goose bumps.

"Here you are, My Lord," my aunt said, coming between us, "your pheasant." Alister removed his hand. Madelaine set down a wooden platter in front of Alister. I usually loved the scent and flavor of the roasted bird, but my stomach felt sick; I fought back bile.

I slid over so Madelaine could sit between us. My uncle leaned forward, pushing his platter where I could see it. "Struck down by my arrow along the way," he boasted. "Would you like a taste?"

"I've already eaten," I replied.

My uncle grinned, pulled the platter back, and began talking to his cousin, Diomat, who sat near him as he carved a hunk of flesh from the bird. He shoved an enormous bite of fowl into his mouth, the crispy golden skin hanging from the corner of his lips. He pressed the morsels into his mouth with his greasy fingers, bloating his checks like a dead thing.

I took a deep breath. I tried to remind myself that it would be Madelaine who would pay if I lost my composure. Or the worse still, that Alister would lose himself again. My head ached.

The food was cleared and the pipers began to play a jig. The smoke burned my eyes. The men—the drunken men—rambled out of the castle to urinate, to vomit, or to take one of the scullery maids. I watched as Aggie passed through the room. One of Alister's men grabbed her and pulled her onto his lap. She smiled and tried to excuse herself, but there was little she could do. Around the pair, everyone laughed. The soldier tickled her chin then stuck his hand down the front of her gown, fondling her breasts. I saw her cheeks flush red.

I turned and looked at Madelaine. She'd already seen and had motioned discreetly to Tavis. The soldier was playing with Aggie's skirts, trying to stick his hands between her legs when Tavis interrupted and called the soldier away. Laughing, he dumped her to the floor when he rose. I watched her get up quickly and hurry back to the kitchen. Her cheeks were wet with tears.

What ladies there were in the room were pulled to their feet. My uncle's cousin Diomat, against my wishes, dragged me to the dance floor. It took all my strength to keep him upright.

"My Lady is quite the beauty," he said, his speech slurring. He stunk like fox piss, the strange gamey scent emanating from his very pores.

My head pounded, and I wondered if all castles kept in such a manner? Would I have to live like this all my life? I noticed Madelaine and Alister moving around the floor. Their words were heated. His hand held the back of her neck tightly. I could see his fingers pressing into her skin. I then noticed someone else's eyes on the pair: Tavis. Commoner born, he had no chance, but he loved Madelaine. I could see from his expression that he was smothering his rage. How horrid to see someone you loved not only with another but to be treated so poorly. I pitied him.

Before I could return to my seat, Lord MacKay, whose wife was not present, asked me to dance.

"Ah, our little lass, how you would love the pageantry of King Malcolm's court! It's a sight to see all those ladies in their fine gowns. They look like flowers strewn in the wind. But they are dainty little birds, not hardy stock like you and your aunt." He droned on and on as we danced, his hands resting too low on my back for my liking. I stepped heavily on his feet and didn't apologize for my clumsiness. When the dance was done, I hurriedly excused myself, fleeing to my chamber.

The house did not hush for many hours, presumably until all the men had passed into drunken unconsciousness. I was trying to sleep when I heard the door open. Terror gripped me, but I turned to see Madelaine in the doorway. She slid into bed beside me. Exhausted, I lay very still. I had just started to fall asleep again when I heard her whimper.

"What is it?" I whispered.

My aunt did not respond. I moved, allowing the moonlight to glide past me onto her swollen face. She held a wet rag against her eye: it was red, puffy, and black. She looked deathly pale.

"Madelaine!" I exclaimed.

"It's nothing," she whispered.

I went to the water basin, moistened a fresh piece of cloth, and took the old one she'd been clutching. I gently pressed the clean cloth against her face.

"Why?" I asked. Rage made my hands shake. Violent anger swelled up in me. I was so angry I realized I bit my tongue. Blood swelled in my mouth, filling my mouth with its salty taste. I felt feverish. I wanted to kill Alister.

Tears rolled down Madelaine's cheeks. "It doesn't matter why. This is what men do. Husbands don't love their wives. They especially do not love wives who bear no children."

I felt sick. I asked said pointedly, "Your miscarriages …did they follow such cruelty?" How many little ones had Madelaine lost? She rarely spoke of it, but I knew she had lost or put into the grave at least six little souls, too many for a mother to count. "He beat you until you lost your children, didn't he? Then beat you again because you bore none? Madelaine, you must not suffer this! Are you to have no happiness?"

"I have found some."

"With Tavis?"

"Well, that is something different. You fill my heart."

"Then I shouldn't go!"

"You must."

"Then come with me."

Madelaine shook her head. "Only nine. Nine is the holy number. Someone else has moved on, and you shall take her place as the new ninth."

"Were you with these women before?"

Madelaine nodded. "The world is changing, Little Corbie. Soon all will follow the White Christ. But all the women in our family go amongst the wise women when their time comes. Some stay for a short time while others train for many years."

"What about you?"

"Scant months thanks to a marriage contract. The family needed an alliance with Alister's clan. I sealed the alliance."

"Then family duty comes before the old ones?"

Madelaine sighed. "You must realize your immediacy to the throne. King Malcolm is your uncle. As well you know, he had only daughters, your cousins, Bethoc and Donalda. While the line of succession will pass to the next male heir, Bethoc's son Duncan, you must realize your importance. Any son you bare will have a claim at the throne. You are a valuable chess piece. They will marry you off to the most royal lord in the land, if not to Duncan himself, to ensure there is no rivalry. But there are many young Lords who would gladly mix their blood with the line of MacAlpin. Your fate is not yours to determine. These scant few years you have before a match is made must be lived with passion. Learn what you can. Be who you truly are."

I didn't want to think about it, but I knew her words were true. I had always known I was meant for a bridal contract. But would they really marry me off to Duncan? My own cousin? Such close matches were not uncommon, I knew, but I shuddered at the thought. Such a marriage would also mean great things for me…I would be Queen of Scots…my sons would be princes.

Nonetheless, my heart sank as I looked at Madelaine. My womb would be used to forge alliances or birth princes. I would never be free, just as she had never been free. We belonged to the crown, and I was a prize like her, waiting to be reaped. I understood then something about the world: legitimacy and power determined your fate.

I sighed then kissed my aunt on her forehead. "I love you."

"I love you too."

I snuggled next to Madelaine and pulled my covers to my chin, my mind spinning. What if they married me to a man like Alister? What would I do with such a man? Outside my window, I heard the call of a raven. It landed on the sill just outside, a mouse in its talons. The mouse's dead, bulging black eyes gleamed in the moonlight. With its sharp beak, the raven ripped its corpse to bits.

Four

THE NEXT MORNING, I AWOKE groggy and starved for fresh air. Madelaine had gone back to her duties. My mind spun with a hundred different ways for Alister to die, but none of them seemed violent enough. I lay in bed and stared out my window. A heavy mist rose. Finally, I pulled on a cloak over my bed clothes and went below.

I crept past the sleeping men in the feasting hall to the garden at the side of the castle. There, in the first of the morning sunlight, I knelt between rows of herbs. No doubt the cooks would soon, though lovingly, chase me away, so I quickly snapped fresh tendrils of mint, thyme, and other herbs. I thought their sweet scent would cheer Madelaine, and I'd often seen her brew the herbs into a draft. She said it calmed her. Something told me she might need them. The leaves were wet with morning dew. My fingers became moist, dirty, and perfumed with the herbs. I held the bunches in my hands and breathed deeply until the heady scent made me feel dizzy. I stuffed the herbs into my pockets and headed toward the front of the castle.

In the field, fire rings puffed up dissipating tails of smoke. The encampment was clearing; the men were heading home. I prayed this meant that the siege of debauchery was over.

As I walked, I spied a small trembling mass sitting near one of the abandoned camps. I climbed a small hill toward it and found a furry black body battling the wind. When I came to stand over her, she looked up at me with her sad brown eyes. It was a tiny puppy. She whimpered softly, rose on her six-inch tall legs, and waddled toward me, her tail wagging. I patted her head. She started licking me, her little pink tongue working hard. I laughed, picking her up and hugging her. She was shivering.

"Poor little thing," I whispered to the pup. "Let's get you inside."

I turned to head back to the castle only to find myself face to face with Father Edwin.

"My Lady, good morning to you! May the Lord bless you this fine morning! Ah, what do you have there?" He was wearing long gray robes, a large wooden cross hanging from his neck. He peered at my hands with his sharp, gray eyes.

I looked away from him. "Just a pup. She was in the field," I said and tried to pass by him, but he moved to stop me.

"A faerie thing then. Let me take it to the men and have its throat slit. You shouldn't bring a foundling inside the castle walls," he said, reaching for the puppy.

I clutched the puppy closer and looked down at her. Her brown eyes met mine. "No," I said sternly and started walking toward the castle. I saw Tavis near the gate. He caught sight of me and began crossing the lawn toward me...and Father Edwin.

Father Edwin turned to walk beside me, still pressing his point. "Such temptations should be avoided, My Lady. The fey folk still play with high-born people such as yourself. Give it to me. I'll be rid of it," he was saying when we met with Tavis.

"What is that, Corbie?" Tavis interrupted, eyeing Father Edwin suspiciously as he stepped closer to me. I moved toward Tavis.

"Just a wee pup."

"I told My Lady that it is the work of the faerie folk to leave such traps for young girls. It should be thrown in the river."

Tavis laughed. "Have you become so suspicious, Priest? Faerie folk? You talk like a superstitious fool, scared of some bitch's abandoned runt. Be off with you."

"But, Lord Tavis," the priest interjected.

"Your master is awake. He'll be looking for you," Tavis said sternly, stepping between me and the priest.

Father Edwin glared at Tavis then turned and headed back into the castle.

"It's early in the day to start an argument with the White Christ, Little Corbie," Tavis said, grinning at me. Clearly, he had not yet seen Madelaine's broken face. I pitied the pain I knew he would feel. I pitied the revenge he would not be able to extract. I pitied his love. But I was grateful for his help.

"That is certain," I said with a wry grin. I set the puppy down. It waddled over to him, its belly bulging.

"So, a foundling, eh? Have you named her?"

I shook my head. "No doubt she already has a one. I just need to figure it out."

Tavis shook his head. "All right," he said with a smile. "But what if it really was the fey folk who left her? Or maybe even the little people of the hollow hills?" he asked jokingly. Laughing, he picked up the pup and was scratching her belly when two of my uncle's men neared us. I caught just a snippet of their conversation.

"They say Duncan may take a wife this year," said the first.

The other man laughed. "Nonsense. He's just a boy. They will wait until they can make a sturdy alliance," the other replied as he mounted.

"With King Cnut badgering Malcolm, no doubt there will be some movement very soon."

"All the movement being done is being done by Thorfinn."

"He's just a welp with a big ship."

"He may be a welp, but he's allied with King Magnus of Norway, and he's fostering Macbeth."

"Shame about Macbeth's father. Findelach was a good man."

Tavis, also overhearing the conversation, cleared his throat loudly. Both men looked at us.

"Ah, Lady Corbie," said the first, winking knowingly to his partner.

The second man turned to me. "And here is Boite's daughter," he said slickly, casting a knowing glance to his comrade.

Tavis handed the puppy back to me. "Farewell, My Lords," Tavis said gruffly, cutting off the words lingering on the men's tongues.

The men laughed knowingly then guided their horses away from the castle, gossiping like two old women as soon as they were out of earshot. I heard my name carry on the wind.

I thought about their words. My cousin Donalda's husband Findelach had been killed by his own brother, Gillacoemgain, in a quarrel over the rule of Moray. Findelach had fallen out of King Malcolm's favor, and it was rumored that the King secretly supported Gillacoemgain's move to take power from his brother. Apparently Macbeth, my second cousin by Donalda, had heard the rumor as well. People said he fled to Lord Thorfinn of Orkney for protection. King Malcom had no problem striking out at his own when it pleased him, much as he'd done to my own father, according to the rumors. My elder cousin Donalda, now a widow, was back at court, and Gillacoemgain, despite killing Donalda's husband, was now the Mormaer of Moray and the most powerful man in the north. I frowned as I thought about where I fit on that chessboard. Would they really marry me off to Duncan? I'd never even seen the boy. The thought of it made me feel indignant, but in the end, the truth was obvious: King Malcolm would move me soon.

Five

FOR THE MEN WHO STILL remained, the revelry began at sunup as opposed to sundown. I spent most of the morning and afternoon playing with the puppy and avoiding the main hall, but by dinnertime, I had no more excuses.

The hall was again too bright. The musicians played too loudly, and the smoke was so thick that it made it hard to breathe. Sweat beaded down my back. The men, still unwashed, were drunk from the day before and continued to drink more. Their speeches slurred.

"This will be the last night. They will all go home tomorrow," my aunt whispered. The salve she had used to hide the bruise around her eye had faded. The dark ring around her shining emerald eyes was obvious. While Madelaine tried to smile like she had no cares in the world, I seethed.

I moved discreetly and forced my body to feel small so no one would notice me. It was difficult, however, to escape attention. My aunt and I were the most fetching women in the room, and when the food had been cleared, the men sought out attractive dancing partners.

"Dance, niece," my uncle said, grabbing my hand.

My aunt, despite the risk of accusation, had taken to the floor with Tavis. I noticed their words were soft as he examined her eye and looked on her sympathetically. They weren't doing a very good job hiding their feelings for one another. And when Tavis looked at Alister, his eyes smoldered. I tried to entertain my uncle, keeping his back turned toward his wife and her lover. I feared for Tavis. His rage was too ready, too obvious. He needed to be smarter. If Alister ever suspected anything between Madelaine and Tavis, Tavis would be dead.

"Such a pretty girl," Alister said then, stroking his rough finger down my cheek.

"Thank you, my uncle," I replied, my stomach flopping with nausea.

He pulled me closer. "How many years have you lived in my house?" he asked, his words coming slow and slurred.

"Sixteen."

"Now you are leaving. And a convent? What a shame! You've grown into such a fine and beautiful woman," he said, his hands stroking slowly upward from the curve of my waist toward my chest.

"Just for a time. King Malcolm will make a match for me soon enough," I said. "I will be given a royal husband and produce heirs for the realm," I said pointedly, reminding Alister that his hands had no business on a body intended for greater things than himself.

He frowned and lowered his hands to my waist. "As a daughter of Boite should."

"Indeed. But, of course, all the realm knows that you are my foster father, and I always think of you as such. I am so glad I bring a father's pride to your eyes."

Alister looked away from me then, and I saw a glimmer of shame cross his face. "Well, if you hope to please your royal husband, don't let those women teach you too much. Take your foster father's advice, and don't become as wicked tongued as your aunt. No man will want you, royal or not."

The harp strings fell silent. "Of course, my uncle and foster father. Many thanks for your good counsel. Let me beg your leave. May I retire to my chamber? The ale has given me a headache."

With a grunting laugh, my uncle nodded dismissively.

It was his words, not the ale, that made my head ache. He made my poor aunt, one of the kindest women I knew, seem wicked. Worse, I knew Alister fully believed in what he said, making his way reality to so many, simply because he thought he could. I shot a knowing glance to Madelaine, who had untangled herself from Tavis before Alister's eyes espied the pair, and headed to my chamber.

Back in the privacy of my own room, I could finally relax. My little puppy was sleeping in a basket at the foot of my bed. She opened her drowsy eyes and looked at me when I entered, her tail wagging.

"Sleep, little one," I told her. "And send me a dream so I can learn your name."

The puppy rolled onto her back, her tongue falling out of the side of her mouth, then drifted back to sleep.

I went to the open window casement and looked out at the silver moon. It was glowing brightly. In the field below, two men where stringing up a freshly killed stag. The light of the fire and the glow of the moon illuminated the scene. I couldn't quite catch their words on the wind, but they were laughing and drinking. I saw the flash of silver as the hunter took out a knife and slit open the belly of the deer with a jerk.

Blood and guts erupted like heavy rain. The deer's intestines burst from the body and with a wet sounding heave, spilled bloody red onto the earth.

The hunter groaned a disgusted grunt as blood splattered all over him.

The image both awed and horrified me. The blood and heap of guts made a massive dark pool at the hunter's feet. The red of innards and blood glimmered in the firelight. The image of it so unsettled me that I swooned. I gazed up at the moon. My head feeling dizzy.

For a brief moment, I saw the world in double vision. Everything around me suddenly felt very far away. I held on to the stone window casement, but my body felt like it was spinning.

The men's voices grew increasingly distant. Everything became dark.

The world glimmered from blackness to a rainbow of opalescent colors then to darkness once again and everything became very still and silent and black. The spinning sensation stopped and my feet were on solid earth, but I didn't know where. The only thing that was certain was that I was not in my chamber anymore.

I saw the light of a fire in the far distance and traveled to it with the speed of thought. I moved as if on the wings of a bird. Propelled through time and space, wings beating in the wind, I soon found myself standing beside a cauldron. A fire was burning underneath. Two women stood aside the fire. One was ancient looking, the lines on her face deeply grooved. The other was more middle-aged; her hair was deep-red.

"Twice the raven has cawed," said the ancient matriarch.

"Twice the star flower has bloomed," said the red-haired woman.

"'Tis time,'tis time," they said together.

"Are you...are you the ladies of the nine?" I asked.

The ancient one laughed a long and heady laugh. "Hail daughter of Boite."

The red-haired woman bowed to me. "Hail Queen hereafter."

"Cauldron queen, old one reborn, come join, come join," they called to me. They joined their hands, extending their free ones to me, motioning for me to join them in their circle.

"Round the cauldron come and sing," said the elder.

"Like fey things in a ring," said the younger.

The hair on the back of my neck rose, and my skin chilled to goose bumps. These were not Madelaine's women. I knew who they were: the Wyrd Sisters. Their dark magic was known only in ancient lore. It was said that they meddled in the world of men. They had not been seen since the time of my ancestor, Kenneth MacAlpin, when their prophecies helped him unite old Alba. My body chilled from head to toe.

"I know who you are," I whispered. "What do you want from me?"

"A deed with a heavy name," answered the ancient one with a laugh.

"A service, Lady," said the younger.

"Nay, nay…say Queen," said the elder.

"But more yet, say Sister," replied the younger, red-haired one.

"Even more," the elder said mysteriously. The old woman let go of her younger companion and drew close to me. She was ancient. As she neared me, the sharp smell of flowers effervesced from her, familiar and sweet. While her words frightened me, her eyes were soft and loving. "Bubble of the earth, and Goddess hereafter," she said then reached up to draw a mark on the center of my forehead. "Wake."

My eyes opened with a jolt. I was lying on my chamber floor staring up at the ceiling. Pain shot through my body. I sat up and touched the back of my head. It was wet. In the dim candlelight, I could see blood on my fingers. I must have fainted.

I rose slowly and glanced outside. The men were skinning the stag. I went over to my water basin to rinse the blood from my fingers, but I gasped when I caught my reflection. One the center of my forehead, drawn in blood, was a flower with five petals. I leaned forward to look at it better. For just a moment, I spied the image of the Wyrd Sisters standing behind me. I turned to see…nothing. And when I peered back into the basin, the vision was gone. The bloody flower, however, remained. I wiped a wet cloth across the symbol, washing away the flower…the symbol of the Cauldron Goddess, the Goddess Cerridwen.

SIX

ON THE MORNING OF THE full moon, Madelaine, Tavis, and I road into the countryside. My pup slept lazily in a sling I'd strapped to my chest. Alister hadn't bothered to wake to see me off, for which I was grateful. We rode past the loch we'd visited just days before. The trees were still loaded with sweet smelling pink and white blossoms. As we rode, I thought about the Wyrd Sisters. Had I really seen them or was it just a dream? The notion that they had appeared to me thrilled and frightened me all at once. After all, the Wyrd Sisters were ladies of legend, dark legend. The Wyrds could be dangerous. Magical beings, they lived in the otherworld. But usually, there were three of them. Where was the third?

"Bid Tavis farewell. We'll travel alone from here," Madelaine called when we reached the stream where I'd met the huntress Madelaine had called Uald.

Tavis smiled sadly at me. "Don't get into too much mischief," he warned.

I smiled at him. His hair shimmered sunflower-yellow in the morning light. "Who? Me?"

Tavis shook his head and turned to Madelaine. "Are you sure you want me to wait for you here? Shouldn't I come deeper into the woods? If anything were to happen to you..."

Madelaine smiled gently at him. Leaning from her horse, she reached out and cupped his chin. "I'll be fine," she said, passing him a wink.

Tavis nodded, but his forehead wrinkled with worry.

"Let's go," Madelaine said. Clicking to her horse, she led us into the woods. After just a few minutes ride, Tavis was out of sight, and we were lost to the forest. Madelaine, however, seemed assured of the path.

"You remember the way," I said, surprised. How long ago had she last come here?

"Somewhat. But even if I'd forgotten, I could follow the pattern of trees," she said, pointing. "Oak, ash, and thorn. Nine oak. Nine ash. Nine thorn. Where things are in nines, you will find the Great Lady."

"Are you sure you can't stay with us? I'm worried about you alone in the castle," I told her. "You are so at peace in the woods. Can't you get away, tell Alister you want to retire to the convent as well?"

She shook her head. "I wish I could. You forget, I am still of breeding age. I'm not my own," she said, and I saw a dark shadow cross her eyes.

"Can't you go to Malcolm? Wouldn't he let you join court life, at least until I am married? Then maybe you can join me?"

Madelaine shook her head. "I've asked...pled. Malcolm knows. He wants me where I am. Please don't worry about me. It's my lot in life, and sick as it is, I've grown used to it. At least you will be away from all the misery." I could tell from the look on her face that talking about it was only making her unhappier, so I stopped.

Madelaine sighed deeply then gazed at the canopy of trees. Blobs of sunlight shone down on her, shimmering off her red hair. Her green riding gown matched the new leaves. I wished she could just run away with Tavis, but she was no freer to love anyone she chose than I was.

Late in the day we came upon a mountain pass that was thick with foliage. In fact, it looked impassable. Madelaine, however, moved toward it.

"There? But it's a tangle," I said.

"Exactly," Madelaine replied with a laugh. "What fool would go in there?" Encouraging her horse, she road into the narrow passage. I followed. Our horses snorted in complaint as we pushed our way through. We passed into what looked like a gap in the mountainside, barely tall enough for the horses to fit. I bent low above my horse's neck so my head wouldn't scrape. On the other side, we emerged into an open space where five small houses sat around an open garden. High mountains and thick, dense, foliage surrounded the space. It was a completely hidden forest grove.

A yellow-haired girl about my age was tending the center fire ring, gingerly pushing kindling onto the fire. Her nimble fingers jumped back when the flames licked them. The woman Madelaine had called Uald, the huntress from the stream, sat beside the fire plucking a bird. A woman with long white hair emerged from one of the houses.

"Greetings in the name of the Goddess," Madelaine called.

"Greetings, daughter," the white-haired woman replied then turned her gaze on me. "Ah, Gruoch. Welcome!" she called.

We dismounted.

The white-haired woman hurried to us. She smiled as she looked me over, chuckling lightly when she saw the pup strapped to my chest. "I'm Epona," she introduced, pulling me into an embrace. The heavy scent of herbs clung to her hair, and her embrace was soft. After she let me go, she turned and gently patted Kelpie's neck.

"Lovely creature. What's his name?" she asked as she leaned in and pressed her cheek against his face, whispering in his ear. To my surprise, my horse nickered softly to her.

"Kelpie," I replied.

Epona smiled. "Are you a Kelpie?" she asked him. He snorted and pawed the earth, causing Epona to laugh. I eyed the woman curiously. Although her hair was pure white, she was not old. Her face was clear and free of wrinkles. Her lips were red, and her eyes were a brownish-gold color. She patted Kelpie one more time then turned and smiled prettily at me. "Uald you have already met," she said with an open hand directed toward the huntress who'd met me at the stream.

"Happy to have you here," Uald said, but she was looking at Madelaine who was grinning at her.

"Come here, child," Epona called to the blonde-haired girl.

The girl dusted her hands off on her skirt and joined us.

"This is Ludmilla. She comes to us from amongst the Rus. Her language is not perfect, but she is learning," Epona said.

Ludmilla smiled at Madelaine and me. "Hello," she said timidly. Her voice was thick with a deep, round accent.

"Gruoch, Elaine, come inside," Epona said then led us toward her cabin.

I raised an eyebrow at my aunt. Elaine?

The air inside Epona's house was thick with the smell of heady white sage. The main room housed a large table at which nine chairs had been set. Epona's bed was tucked into a small room in a back corner of the house. The floor had been laid with a rough stone and was covered with soft straw.

"Everything is the same," Madelaine commented.

"Yes, but you'll only know Uald and I. The ones who were here with you have gone, been replaced by other adepts," Epona replied.

"I heard that Dahlia, as she was called, is in Powys," Madelaine said.

Epona nodded and poured a yellow liquid from a wooden decanter into three glasses. "The others are dispersed from the north beyond the Hadrian's Wall all the way south to Brittany." She handed a glass to me and Madelaine then took one for herself.

"Have any gone to the other groves? The other covens of nine? There was a girl, I don't recall her name, with periwinkle-colored eyes," Madelaine said, then turned to me. "We all thought she was part fey. Magical thing. What ever happened to her?"

Epona smiled. "She is in service at the forest coven. You see, my dear," Epona said, turning to me, "we are nine here. But there are, in total, nine strongholds of the Goddess spread across the old country, each always with a count of nine. We keep the sacred ways...in secret, of course."

I looked at Madelaine. What other secrets had she been keeping?

"Drink," Madelaine said with a laugh.

I took a sip. The liquid was like nothing I had ever drunk before; I grimaced at the bitter taste and tried not to spit it out. I was embarrassed by my rudeness, but no one noticed.

Epona peered at Madelaine's bruised face. "Still at it, is he?" she asked. "I'd hoped someone would have killed him by now." Setting her glass down, she turned and dipped into her wooden cupboard. Inside were a multitude of glass jars and some dried herbs lying in baskets. "The nettles were strong this year." She handed Madelaine a small green jar filled with salve.

With a nod, Madelaine stuck it into the pocket of her coat.

Epona patted Madelaine's shoulder sympathetically, but I saw a flash of anger cross her face. She then turned and looked at me, her hand on her hip. "Well, do you like the drink?"

"Yes," I lied.

Epona chuckled. "Dispense with formalities. We speak the truth here. I know it tastes like stump water. It will give you prophetic dreams. In it are herbs that prompt visions of the future."

I smiled at Epona. I liked her already.

Uald entered behind us, wiping her hands with a rag.

"Will you help Gruoch get settled while I speak with Elaine?" Epona asked Uald.

"Corbie," Madelaine said then. "Most people call her Corbie...she's my little raven."

"Suits her well," Epona replied. "Very well, Corbie, please go with Uald while I shamelessly shake news from Madelaine," she added with a laugh.

Uald nodded and motioned for me to follow her. Without another word, I rose and went back outside.

The puppy stirred at my chest. Stopping, I set her down. She ran straight to Ludmilla. The girl smiled and patted the little scamp. Uald and I started unbundling my horse.

"Armaments?" she asked, poking at the bulky packages.

"Madelaine sent them for you," I replied. I hadn't understood Madelaine's gift when she had Tavis pack my horse, but the more I studied Uald, the more sense it made. Uald grinned happily, her smile pulling toward one side of her face. She was pretty in a rough kind of way. She was nearly the same age as Madelaine, but I saw some tendrils of white streaking her hair. Her skin was tanned from the sun and there was a scattering of freckles on her nose and cheeks. Her eyes were very dark brown, her reddish-brown hair pulled back in a braid. As she did when she called me in the woods, she wore breeches and a tunic. Her arms curved with the muscles of a smith. I could tell from the cut of her that she was a swordswoman. No wonder Madelaine had sent her weapons.

With my arms fully loaded, I followed Uald into one of the little houses. Inside there were two small beds, a small wooden table, two wardrobes, and two chests. Uald set the packages down on one of the beds.

"You'll share this house with Ludmilla."

I pulled a chain mail vest and a green gown from my belongings. I handed them to Uald. "These are also for you."

Uald frowned at the dress. "She always wanted me in gowns. I never saw the point," she said but took it all the same. "Why don't you get settled? I'll come back for you in a while; the others will be anxious to meet you," Uald said then left. She carried the bundle of armaments strapped across her back and the chainmail over her shoulder. The dress, however, she held in her hands, studying it as she walked toward the barn. I saw the bemused expression on her face.

I stood in the doorframe and watched Ludmilla with the pup. Seeing me standing in the door of her home, Ludmilla came toward me. The puppy waddled along behind her.

"You sleep here?" Ludmilla asked.

I smiled and nodded.

Ludmilla looked at my packages. "You a queen?"

Confused, I shook my head. "No."

Now it was her turn to look puzzled. "Such beautiful things. Epona says you a queen."

"I am no queen."

Ludmilla laughed then shrugged.

I opened the trunk at the end of the bed and lay a bear fur on the bottom. The puppy hopped and hopped, trying to get on my bed. Taking pity on her, I set her on top before unloading all my dresses and other belongings into the trunk. I watched Ludmilla's eyes widen at what I thought were the plainest of my clothes. I pulled a red gown with an embroidered collar from my things. "This dress no longer fits," I lied. "Would you like to have it?" I asked, handing it to Ludmilla.

"I sew for you?"

I shook my head. "No, you have it."

Again, she smiled. "Thank you...Gruoch?" she asked, seeing if she was pronouncing my name correctly.

"Please, call me Corbie." I smiled back. "Where are the other ladies?"

Ludmilla slid across my bed and looked out the window. "Two is collecting herbs," she said, pointing to a dense area behind one of the little houses. "The old one sleeps. Another is away, and I don't know where is the other." Epona was right, Ludmilla's language was still a bit broken, but I still understood her well.

A moment later, the two women collecting herbs emerged from the woods.

"You meet them," Ludmilla said and rose. I followed her.

When I exited the house, the two women looked in my direction. They smiled at one another when they saw me.

"Welcome, Lady Gruoch," the taller woman with long brown hair called. She was very thin and had a Roman looking nose. Her eyes were pale blue. She wore a long, well-worn gray-colored gown covered by a long apron with many pockets. Small tufts of leaves and twigs stuck out of the pockets. She smiled at me, but her gaze was cool. Something inside me froze against her, and I wondered why.

"Indeed, welcome," the second woman, who was much shorter, added. Her blonde, curly hair was cropped at her neck. The dark blue gown she wore complemented her eyes which were almost exactly the same shade as her gown. "I'm Aridmis."

"Druanne," the first woman with lighter blue eyes said, nodding to me.

"Thank you both. Please, call me Corbie." Suddenly, I felt a little overwhelmed by all the new names and faces.

Druanne peered closely at me, her eyes crinkling at the corners. "All right...Lady Corbie."

Aridmis gave her a sharp look.

Puzzled, I frowned and looked around the camp; there was no sign of the other women.

"They will join us shortly, no doubt," Druanne said, as if reading my thoughts. "Except Tully. She's currently travelling."

I raised a questioning eyebrow at her. She smiled smugly and looked away from me.

Epona and Madelaine emerged from Epona's house. I could tell from the expression on Madelaine's face that it was time for her to go. Her eyes were watery.

I crossed the lawn and took her hand. "So soon?"

She nodded sadly.

Uald came from the barn leading Madelaine's horse. "He drank his weight in water and got a good nibble of oats," she told Madelaine. Uald too looked sad.

"You can't stay the night?" I asked Madelaine.

She shook her head.

The door to a nearby house opened. A very old woman exited. I had to look twice. She resembled the old woman I had seen in my vision, the ancient-looking Wyrd Sister, but it was not her.

"Bride," Epona called to the elder woman, raising her voice. "Meet our new sister."

The old woman, whose silver hair was pinned in a loose bun, came toward me, her arms outstretched. "Welcome, child," she said and took hold of both of my arms which she squeezed gently.

"Greetings, Mother. I'm Corbie."

"Oh, I wondered what all the fuss was about. I sleep most afternoons. I am a crone, you see," she added with a laugh.

When Bride was done, Madelaine embraced me, kissing my cheek. "If you need me, I can come. It will not be hard to send word. They will teach you," she whispered in my ear.

I held my aunt close. Tears fell from my eyes, but I tried to steel myself. I didn't want the others, particularly Druanne, to see. Something told me I shouldn't show her my weaknesses. We held our embrace for a long time. Eventually Madelaine pulled away.

"I love you," I whispered quietly to her.

"And I you," she replied, kissing me on the forehead. Uald helped Madelaine mount her horse then, holding the reigns, led Madelaine to the small crevice in the rock wall. When she neared the passage, Uald kissed Madelaine's hand, passed her the reins, and turned and headed back toward the barn. Madelaine turned once more to wave to me, then rode into the jumble of rocks that hid the enclosure, leaving me to a life all new.

seven

"COME. THERE IS MUCH TO discuss," Epona said. She took my hand and led me around the back of her house. We followed a worn path through the woods.

"I want to tell you a few things so you feel more comfortable and understand more of what will happen in the next few days," she explained. "First, you will be renamed. This is the hardest for some to deal with so I want you to get used to the idea. Also, let me tell you why you will be renamed. Here, we worship the Goddess. The names we take are our Goddess names. We take them in service of the Great Mother. Do I need to explain her to you?"

I shook my head. We all knew the mother of the land, the lady of the earth and hunt. She was our Goddess before the White Christ came.

"You will be renamed according to which aspect of the Goddess best fits you. It will be your Goddess name. Use it only amongst us. Your name is special and powerful. Anyone who knows your true name holds power over you. All of the other women here have been renamed except Ludmilla. Like you, Ludmilla has not had a renaming ceremony. I was named Epona because of my love of horses. As well, medicine, fertility, crops, language and divination all fall under my thumb.

"Uald is named for a Goddess who was a weaponsmith, a hunter, a forester. Druanne, as is obvious from her name, is Druid-taught. She is one of the last of the old kind. Aridmis is of the silver wheel; she reads the heavens. Bride, named for the cheerful spirit of the spring maid inside her, now belongs to the Crone. She has performed the Croning ceremony, an ancient ritual done by women who have ceased their menses. Taith, who we call Tully, you have not met. She is our scout. She travels from hidden coven to hidden coven, keeping a network amongst us alive. She won't be back for several months," Epona explained.

"And the ninth?"

Epona and I reached a spring that ran out of the side of one of the steep hills surrounding the grove. The water fell first onto a little rocky ledge and then into a large pool that was several feet deep. Coins and jewels lay on the ledge.

"Feel free to drink or bathe here, but give thanks to Anwyn, the lady of this spring, when you do."

Bending down, I pulled a small silver band from my pinky and laid it under the water with the rest of the treasures. In my mind, I whispered a greeting to the Goddess and then took a drink. The water was cool and metallic tasting. It felt icy as it slid down my throat.

Epona drank as well, offering a whispered prayer under her breath.

A rustling came from the brush nearby, and much to my surprise, a woman with brown hair that stretched to her feet fell out of the bushes. Dressed in a mishmash of animal skins and woven cotton clothing, she looked wildly about her and appeared to be talking to the incorporeal air. Her hair was knotted and full of leaves and twigs. Her face, while beautiful, was very dirty. She stopped suddenly as if someone had addressed her and, turning her head quickly, she looked at Epona and me.

"Our ninth. I wanted you to meet her without the other women around," Epona said quietly. "She is… different," she added then, turned to the woman. "Come, Sid. Meet your new sister."

The woman she called Sid rushed toward us. When she reached the spring she fell to her knees. Muttering, she took a quick drink from the spring then looked up at me, water dripping from her chin.

"Darkness has come. They saw you near the loch," the woman said to me.

I raised an eyebrow at her. "At the loch? I saw no one at the loch."

Sid laughed, her eyes glimmering. "The dragonflies…of course, they were not *really* dragonflies…it was their sharp eyes that spotted you when you came the first time with Mad Elaine. They were afraid you would fly down with your raven beak and snatch them up. And you picked snowdrops, which made them afraid."

Puzzled, I didn't know what to say.

She took advantage of my silence. "They've seen her flying," she told Epona.

"To where?"

"Through the night. On the silver thread."

"Yes, but to where did they see her go?"

"They will not say. They say," Sid said, then paused and tilted her ear as if to listen, "that you will learn soon enough."

Epona frowned.

"They will forgive you for taking up snowdrops if you will leave them cream tonight and come with me to the barrow at sunup," Sid told me.

I looked to Epona.

She nodded. "Fine."

"Ah, darkness, they hear your cries already. But you are an avenger, so what can you do?" Sid asked. She hopped from stone to stone across the small creek to me. She came close beside me and took my hand. She looked at me with sympathy. "I love them but they knot my hair," she whispered in my ear. She stopped and looked suddenly at her shoulder. "Not you, love, the brownies."

"Where have you been?" Epona asked her.

"The Seelies are holding court."

I knew the brownies. They were the riders of the pine marten; they were the six-inch-high brown-haired fey. And there was not a child alive who didn't know who the Seelies were. They were the fair-folk of the mound, the barrows, the place this strange woman wanted to take me the next morning. They were the faerie people who had walked the land before our kind—mankind—had come.

"What of the Unseelies?" Epona asked.

Sid sighed heavily. "First they would not come, though they thought they might. Then they sent Rhiannon. Then they all came. It was a joyous and merry event. We celebrated a good many days."

We turned again and headed back toward the houses.

"Sister, you must be sure to eat. We'll join in the house at sundown. Be sure to come," Epona told Sid when we reached grove.

Sid nodded. "I am told my house is a mess and mischief will be afoot if I do not clean it."

Without another word, Sid rushed off speaking harshly with…her shoulder. Ludmilla, who'd gone back to working on the fire, watched Sid skeptically.

"Well?" Epona asked me. She looked in the direction of Sid.

She seemed mad. Talking with apparitions, dressed like a mad woman, speaking of old things, Sid showed all the signs of madness. Yet by the old ways deep within me, I knew she was not crazy. "She is in communication with the faeries."

"Sid was a victim," Epona said as she sat down on a wooden bench in front of her house. "To the normal eye, she does appear mad. Long ago, a courtly lady took pity on her. They found Sid when she was just a girl, naked, in the woods. She was taken to court, cleaned up, and sent to the kitchens. Sid spoke hardly at all, and when she did speak, it was in this same distracted manner. The lord of the house took kindly to her form, I'm sure you noticed she is striking under all that mess, and begot a bastard child on her. She birthed the child then bashed it on the hearth until it was dead. She was taken from the castle, flogged, and sold to a group of traveling entertainers. They kept her in a cage; she was left talking nonsense as she did in the beginning, and people paid a price to see her. They tortured her for amusement. She still bears scars.

"I found her on one excursion into Wales. I purchased her, mended her wounds, and brought her back with me. It took me awhile to help her reconcile what she saw and the voices she heard to what I, and you, see in this world. She has bridged a large gap.

"Her trips to the other side, however, leave her physical body in a state of disrepair. She has been gone nearly two weeks. I doubt she has eaten human food. When you go with her to the barrow tomorrow, be prepared for an unusual experience," Epona told me.

"About the child she killed. I understand her anger, but—" I was aghast.

"Perhaps, one day, she will tell you the tale, and you can decide for yourself how you feel about such an act," Epona said with a sigh. "She has born another child since. It was, she tells me, to the Seelie King. I saw the child after it was born but have not seen it since. She tells me he lives with his father."

"You don't travel where she goes?"

Epona shook her head. "No one has ever been able to follow Sid."

I nodded. My competitive urge splashed up.

"Ah, I see it in your eyes. I hope you can. Sid would thank you for it."

Uald joined us. "Perhaps we should see to your horse now?"

I nodded and stood.

"Come for dinner thereafter," Epona said and went within.

I followed Uald to the little wooden barn that sat on the right of the grove entrance. A small, fenced pasture was behind the barn; two mares grazed there. Toward one side of the barn was a smithy with stone half-walls and a wooden roof. Behind it was a little room where, it seemed, Uald stayed.

"I do metal working. Are you interested in such things?" Uald asked.

"I'd love to learn."

"I'd love to teach you…Elaine's foster daughter. If you ever need anything, want anything, you can always come to me. Your aunt is very special to me," Uald told me with a smile then pushed the wide barn door open. I led Kelpie inside. The other animals neighed excitedly at the sight of a stallion. My horse, smelling the mares around him, pranced and snorted. I grinned at the lot of them and then put Kelpie out to pasture to meet his new friends.

We left the horses to their prancing and went into the smithy. Uald had been busy hammering spoons and swords. Metal tools hung from the walls and rafters and equipment sat lined up neatly on a table. Carefully piled wood and kindling for the large fire pit lined the wall.

"I sell some of what I make in exchange for the things we need," Uald said, then lifted a sword off her workbench. It was a fine weapon. The hilt had been decorated with engraved leaves.

"It's beautiful."

"I made a dagger for your father once. It must have taken me a hundred casts to get it right. I molded a small raven figure to sit on the hilt. Did you ever see it?"

I thought back, scant images of my father bubbling up in my memory. I did remember him having a fine dagger he wore on his belt. "Maybe…"

"I always wondered what happened to that dagger. I hoped you had it. Perhaps it will find its way home to you some day."

I smiled. It was easy to see why Madelaine, who, like me, had grown up with genteel ladies, liked Uald. I doubted that she had any patience for talk of babes and sewing. "Did you know my father?" I asked.

Uald smiled, her lips pulling into a smirk again. She looked away from me and stared out into the forest. She smiled then nodded. I could tell her mind was busy. "Boite the raven. Yes, I knew him well, but that's a tale for another day. Come on," she said, then led me back to Epona's house.

The sky was turning red. I couldn't believe the day had passed so quickly. Night was coming, and I could feel it in my bones. The puppy scampered from the door frame of my new home. I picked her up and carried her to Epona's house.

Sid emerged from her cottage. She had rid herself of her furs and wore a plain gray dress that was far too large for her. Her hair, however, remained as I had seen it earlier. I set the pup down and joined Uald in washing my hands in a basin near the door. The fuzzy pup went to Sid.

"Oh my, oh my," she said as she bent down to scratch the pup's head. "Better get a talisman," she said to Epona who stood in the open doorway.

The white-headed woman nodded.

"Why?" I asked.

"Oh, the little meddlers are always up to mischief," Sid said then scolded her shoulder. "No, no, not you."

Inside, Ludmilla, Druanne, Aridmis, and Bride had already seated themselves. I sat beside Sid. Her face looked quite sunken, and her body was very thin. Despite her peculiarities, or perhaps because of them, I found I liked her both instantly and intensely.

Epona, who had taken the head seat, looked at each of us and then bowed her head. I followed her in the gesture.

"Mother, we thank you for providing us with food, and we thank you for bringing our ninth to us. Guide us in your will. Protect Tully, who is far from us. Use us, Mother, for your ends. We are your daughters. Blessed be."

The women stirred, and I opened my eyes. I was filled with warmth and light, the comforts of the hearth. They passed flatbread and crocks of stew around the table. Honeyed butter perfumed the room. Everything looked and smelled wonderful.

"I hope this meager food is to your taste, My Lady," Druanne said then.

At first I did not realize she was speaking to me. Everyone at the table grew still. I looked up to find Druanne's eyes on mine.

"You must be used to more sophisticated tastes," she added. She smiled weakly at me, but her eyes were cold.

I saw Uald shift uncomfortably. She passed a glance to Epona, but the white-haired woman held her tongue.

"Nothing tastes better than a meal made by the loving hands of a mother or sister," I replied, feeling the warmth I'd felt only moments before leave me. What reason did this woman have to dislike me? I'd only just arrived.

"Droll, droll. Like a beetle clicking. Pick a new tune, Druanne," Sid said then shoved a bite of bread into her mouth.

Uald chuckled.

Aridmis cleared her throat. "When will we begin planning for Beltane?" she asked Epona.

Druanne looked away.

Epona smiled. "Is your blood stirring?"

"Me?" Aridmis said with a laugh that sounded like a chiming bell. "If I recall correctly, last year it was you who disappeared with that bald-headed Druid into the night."

Everyone, save Druanne, giggled.

"True," Epona said. "True enough," she said with a wink. "You're right. We should begin our plans. Balor and his men, including a new student, will be coming for the festivities. I have also asked the bards of the North to return. They seemed pleased at the invitation."

"Of course they were pleased," Uald grunted.

"Who is Balor's new student?" Bride asked.

"A very promising acolyte; his name is Banquo."

"Will you be here, Sid?" Aridmis asked.

"I should, but you know the barrows."

"So when you say you'll be back at Beltane it means we'll see you at the festival of Lughnassadh?" Uald said with a laugh.

Sid grinned at Uald.

"Will we have a maypole?" Ludmilla asked.

Druanne nodded. "As is customary. Pardon me, Epona, but I have already put together a list of tasks that need to be completed for the celebration. I will, however, need to make some adjustments since I didn't know you invited additional guests."

Epona only smiled then turned to me: "Druanne is in charge of the holiday celebrations. As one of the last female acolytes of the Druidic ways, she can best teach you the mysteries of the high holy days," Epona told me.

"When will I begin her training?" Druanne asked Epona.

"She is going with Sid tomorrow, so I don't know when she will be back. When she returns, however, I'd like to place her in Uald's care until Beltane. By then, Ludmilla and Corbie will both be ready for their name-taking."

"She will begin with Uald? Are you sure that is the wisest—"

"That is what we shall do," Epona replied, cutting Druanne off.

Sid, arguing with the phantom of her shoulder, distracted us all. After some heated discussion she said, "I am told Corbie's goddess has already revealed herself, that she already has a name."

Epona set her spoon down. "And?"

Sid frowned.

"They won't tell you?"

Sid shook her head.

"Come, Nadia, tell us," Epona said, addressing Sid's shoulder.

"They are forbidden to speak," Sid answered.

"Who dares forbid our Good Neighbors?" Epona asked, looking very upset.

The other women looked from Epona, to me, to Sid.

I listened.

"You know who. Who has the courage and power to dare?" Sid replied then turned back to her food.

Epona looked at me then frowned. "Well, we will learn soon enough."

One by one, each of the sisters departed after their meal. Druanne, I noticed, left in a huff without speaking to the others. Bride was still finishing her meal and chatting with Uald and Epona when I rose to leave. I filled a cup with a little cream, as Sid had suggested, then wished everyone goodnight.

Outside, I spotted Aridmis sitting at the side of the well. She held a large piece of parchment in her hands and was drawing on it as she looked toward the heavens.

"What do you see in those stars for me, seer?" I jested.

"Under what moon where you born?"

"I was born of the water bearer in the year 1010."

"Let me look," Aridmis said and peered into the night's sky. She scribbled on her paper. "What do you want to know, fair or foul?"

I shrugged. "Often, what's fair is foul and foul is fair."

"You will wear a crown "

"A crown?" Quite involuntarily my hand drifted toward my head.

"It's not so bad a fate," she said, looking again to her papers.

"But wed to whom? To Duncan?"

Aridmis smiled. "That I can't quite see. But I do know one thing about Duncan."

"What's that?"

"He should beware of valkyries."

Speechless, I stood quietly at her side for several minutes.

"Goodnight, sister," Aridmis said, looking up. Her voice prompted me from my stillness.

"Yes, goodnight."

I would wear a crown. What crown? At the side of what king? My mind boggled at the idea.

That night I dreamed I lay in Sid's bed and cried. I saw Epona's white hair and could hear her comforting voice, but I could not see what was the matter. All I knew was that I was hurt. Some part of my body ached terribly, and the room seemed very hot. It seemed to me that Madelaine was there, but I could not be certain. I heard Druanne chanting, her dry droning voice calling the Goddess. My body was soaked with sweat.

Then the pain cleared, and I was in a soft bed with rich coverings. I rolled over to find a pure white back in my face, masculine muscles curving smoothly. My hands roved upon his skin. The man turned to look at me. He had raven black hair and clear blue eyes, and those eyes were filled with love.

eight

"WAKE UP," SOMEONE SAID, JIGGLING my shoulder. I opened my eyes to see Sid's face peering into mine. She was leaning through the window. I hadn't noticed the day before how delicate her features were. Her nose was small and pinched. Her green eyes sparkled from under long lashes. Her small mouth was rosy pink.

"Hurry and dress. We must race the sun," she whispered.

I looked out the window behind her. It was still mostly dark, but the sun was on its way. I rose quickly and pulled on my boots, not stopping to dress in a fresh gown. Leaving my pup to the warm bed, I crept outside. Ludmilla stirred but did not wake.

Sid rounded the house and began to walk quickly toward the woods. "They liked the cream. You are forgiven."

"What's wrong with snowdrops?" I asked as I tried to wipe the sleep from my eyes. Suddenly, I felt as if my hair had been pulled. "Ouch!"

"Oh, you," Sid said disdainfully, "don't blame people for ignorance," Sid scolded someone directly in front of her. "She's sorry."

"Who?"

"Nadia."

"And Nadia is..." I asked, rubbing my head.

"A fairy. Don't you see her? No, no one does. But, she's right there," Sid said waving her hand in front of her as she marched quickly through the forest.

"Sorry, Nadia. Please be patient with me," I said as I hurried to keep up with Sid. Whoever the phantom Nadia was, I was very certain I wanted to be on good terms with her.

Sid laughed. "You're making friends." She moved quickly over beds of fern and through thickets. Then, as if remembering that she had not answered my question, she said, "Snow drops are poison to fairies. They can't go near them. If you ever fear an evil fey has fallen upon you, take up snowdrops."

Sid kept one eye on the sky and another on the woods ahead of her. The sun was moving quickly upward. We moved through the forest with great haste.

"Sid, how will I be able to follow you?"

"You can ride the silver thread. Do it the same as you did before."

"How do you know about that?"

Sid didn't answer me.

I continued, "And, besides, I did it by accident."

She looked over her shoulder at me. "There is no such thing as accidents. Do it on purpose this time."

"And if I cannot?"

"Then you cannot."

I turned and looked behind me. The village was out of sight, and no clear path returned to it. I was at Sid's mercy.

We entered a valley where the ground was covered by a vast bed of moss, a barrow in the center. Domed like a turtle shell, it rose some eight feet high. It, too, was covered in lichen. Save its shape, it blended into the land, was part of the earth. The mounds were magical places. Many of the barrows were burial mounds. Ancient kings and queens and powerful bards and druids had been buried within. The mounds were places where the worlds were thin. They were places where the faerie folk and beings from the other world crossed the border between our world and theirs, just as they did with the standing stones.

"Come on, Raven Beak," Sid called as she charged right toward the barrow. Pushing some fern boughs away, she revealed a hole the size of a man in the barrow's side. Grinning madly at me, she slid into the hole. Her feet hung outside for only a moment, and then she disappeared.

"Are you coming?" she called from within the barrow.

I balked.

"Quickly!" she added.

Frowning, I wiggled into the hole.

Sid's hands found mine, and she pulled me through. It was terribly dark and I felt, not scared, but ill at ease.

We both paused and let our eyes become accustomed to the darkness. After a few moments, the pre-dawn light coming from the small hole dimly illuminated the space, and I could see more clearly. I gasped as I saw a skeleton lying on an alter in the center of the barrow. It appeared to be female. There were heaps of silver trinkets at her feet.

"Don't mind Boudicca. She won't hassle you, of all people."

I stared at the skeleton lying on the stone alter. "Is it really her?" I asked and took a step toward her. "The ancient Queen? Is it really her?" My skin cooled to goose bumps.

Sid laughed. "Don't you remember this place? Well, maybe you wouldn't. You were riddled with fever from that axe wound when we brought you here, accursed Romans, but I stayed beside you until you passed. Seems I can't get far from this place."

"Romans? What are you talking about? I've never been here before," I said, but my mind bubbled up with terrible images, memories of it. A small party walked with me, carrying torches, as we headed toward the mound. I was limping, holding my side. It ached terribly. Blood had squished through my fingers. I remembered knowing I was dying. I remembered sweating, and feeling sick, and pain. And I remember my terrible fear, not for myself, but for my daughters who I would leave behind.

"Yes, you have. Long ago," Sid said, motioning to the bones on the alter. "What other proof do you need? Here you are. I begged them to wall me in with you, to slit my throat. I wanted to stay with you...you, when you were Boudicca. The last time we were together. You don't remember?"

I saw Sid in a flash of double vision. She had the same face, but her hair was long and very pale-blonde-colored. She was dressed like a warrior. I saw her leaning over me, tears streaming down her cheeks. In my memory, I reached up to touch her face. Blood marred her pretty looks. She removed her helmet and laid her head on my chest. After that, there was nothing. Everything went black. I closed my eyes.

"Sid?" I whispered, feeling myself swoon.

Sid laughed.

"There is a chain between us. Never to be broken. We have been and will always be together. You've just forgotten. Now, keep those eyes closed. Concentrate on the fey," she whispered. "Believe that they exist. Know that the portal to their world lies here. Try to hear them." Her voice began to trail off. "When you are ready, open your eyes, and you will see the portal. Enter. I'll wait on the other side."

I stilled for several moments, concentrating, and then opened my eyes. I watched Sid walk into a shimmering halo of green light. She entered the light and disappeared. Trembling, I moved toward the portal, but it evaporated before my eyes. Everything went dark. Now there was nothing. I stood in the spot where Sid had passed through the portal. Nothing. I swore I could hear Sid's voice in a whisper. I closed my eyes and tried to concentrate.

"See me," I heard Sid beckon. "See me."

I felt power surge up in me. It was a strange, tingly feeling. I opened my eyes. Green light glimmered before me, illuminating the cavern, shining its light on the bones of the dead queen. When I turned to look on the skeleton, the green light faded, and I couldn't hear Sid anymore.

"Sid?" I called. A deep, empty silence fell all around me. My skin crept. "Sid? Sid, can you hear me?"

No answer came. I closed my eyes and tried to concentrate again, but anxiety wracked me. I was too late. A glimmer of sunlight slanted though the hole in the side of the barrow. The sun had risen.

I puzzled at what to do. I was certain I couldn't get back to the grove on my own. Distraught, I sat by the hole and stared at the bones. My hands were shaking. My comrade, who swore we knew each other in lives past, had just disappeared into the world of the fey, and I was alone with bones—my own? I felt the Otherworld pungently around me, more strongly than I had ever felt it before. My skin chilled to goose bumps. My head began to feel very dizzy. The darkness around me felt heavy. I closed my eyes and heard the wings of a bird. Wings. My wings. Raven wings. I felt myself fly though the darkness.

"You're halfway there," a voice said.

Startled, I opened my eyes. I was sitting with my back against a wide gray column. Before me stood the Wyrd Sisters.

"Welcome back," the older woman said.

The world around me was very dark.

"Sid?" I called. I rose to my feet and tried to look around. "Sid?"

"Sidhe is not here, though she is close," the old woman said.

"Come, come to the cauldron," the younger woman said.

"Come, Cerridwen," the ancient matriarch called, motioning me forward.

The younger, red-haired woman frowned. "Not too much or Epona will hide her away."

"Bah, Epona will do as the Goddess commands."

"Cerridwen...why call me by the name of the Welsh Cauldron Goddess?" I demanded.

"Welsh!" the elder woman declared in disgust. "The Goddess of the Cauldron is eternal. She is known by many names...Cerridwen, Hecate, Astarte...all ladies of war and magic, all the same divine creature...all just like you."

I frowned at her. Her answer felt like a riddle. "Why have you brought me here?"

The younger woman with the deep red hair grinned at me. "You tell us. Why have you come here?"

"I was in the barrow."

"But your path ends here," the red-haired woman said.

"Yet still, you are right, Epona will keep her too long," the older woman complained.

"Epona can smell the magic on her, but that is not why Epona keeps her."

"You're right. It is Crearwy she desires."

"And the other."

"Look in your cauldron. The boy belongs to the world. Don't you see the crown on his head?"

The women became silent, their eyes flicking back toward me.

"Come, Cerridwen. I will show him to you. I know you wish to see him," said the elder.

"Who?"

"The man in your dream. Your raven-haired man with skin like snow and eyes the color of the sky," said the younger.

"Your King," added the elder.

Curiosity got the better of me. I stepped forward and looked in the cauldron. He was there, the man from my dream just the night before. He was in battle. I gasped. Many men were upon him, but a blond-haired giant, swinging a massive battle axe, cleared them away. My heart stilled. The women were watching me, but I didn't care. I watched as the raven-haired man moved through the battlefield. He was beautiful. His clear blue eyes sought out his enemy. His cheeks were flushed red from battle vigor.

I reached out and touched his image in the cauldron. The liquid did not ripple like water; it felt soft like silk. I was surprised when the man stopped and looked around him.

"Can you feel me?" I asked.

"Yes," he answered.

"Where are you?" I whispered.

"Caithness."

"Can you see me?"

He shook his head. Then a fierce warrior came upon him. Hearing my voice had caused him to be off his guard. The huge man beat him down, forcing him to hide under his shield, and his blond-haired protector was nowhere in sight.

"No," I yelled. "No!"

I suddenly found myself floating above the battlefield. Below me my raven-haired man and his foe struggled. I flew downward and knocked the foe away. My black-haired man rose and stabbed his enemy. He turned to face me, and it was clear he could see me.

From behind me, someone shouted my name: "Gruoch!"

I turned to see Sid. I was then pulled with a dizzying force back to the cauldron.

"What do you have in the cauldron today? Eye of newt? Toe of frog?" Sid seethed at the Wyrd Sisters.

"Peace, Sidhe," said the ancient one.

Sid took my hand. "Come."

"Come again, Cerridwen," the younger woman called to me. "You are welcome here amongst your sisters."

"Hecate watches. Don't tangle the webs of fate too soon," Sid chided them.

Sid led me forward into the darkness. Moments later, we emerged in the barrow near the alter of Boudicca.

"Our roads take us to different places in the other realm," Sid whispered.

The barrow was dark. "Is it night?"

"Two days later."

"How?"

"That is the way of the Otherworld."

"What do those women want from me?"

"The Dark Goddess is an angry Goddess. Her anger at losing her people to the White Christ makes her seethe. She is full of fury, battle, vengeance, and secret magic.

She is the queen of darkness and night. Those women, and you, wear her face...Cerridwen," she whispered.

"It is my father's curse."

"It is not a curse. Call her what you will, Scotia, Morrigu, Hecate, you belong to her. It is a rare coven. They are the most powerful beings in this land. And they want you. You will be an avenger, as the fey have said."

"Must I go to them? They say Epona is keeping me."

"Epona knows the will of the Goddess as sure as they know it. And she will do what she must. But first, you must learn to be in the seat of power, not riding alongside. We will train you."

"Sidhe," I whispered, repeating the name the elder of the Wyrd Sisters had called Sid.

She grinned. "It's just a name. I won't be impressed until you remember what you called me when you were Boudicca. Come on. I'm starving! I hope Epona has something sweet in her cupboards."

I shook my head and grinned at her. My mind spinning, I followed Sid down a path between nine oak trees back to the coven.

WHEN WE ENTERED THE GROVE, we found that all the houses were dark save Epona's. As soon as we stepped into the clearing, Epona opened her door and beckoned us within.

On the table, several scrolls were rolled out, and I eyed them as Epona dipped into her cupboards. She emerged with bread and dried fruit.

"How are you both?"

"We are intact," Sid replied.

"Did she follow?" Epona asked Sid.

Sid looked at me. "She did go to the other side."

"To the Good Neighbors?"

Sid shook her head. "The Wyrds. I told them that they weave the threads of fate too soon."

Epona nodded. "They are anxious." She then turned to me. "So what have your sisters shown you in the cauldron?"

I balked.

"Come, girl."

"A man," I answered.

Epona looked thoughtful. "Have you seen this man before?"

"Peace, Lady. We've not eaten in days," Sid said as she sliced bread for us both.

Relieved, I exhaled deeply. I didn't even know what I had seen or what it meant. Something about Epona told me that she was trustworthy, that I was safe with her. But the Wyrd Sisters also warned that Epona had her own agenda, and I had no idea what that was. I wasn't sure what to tell her.

Epona softened. "You know my concerns."

Sid nodded.

"Tomorrow, go to the smithy and work with Uald," Epona said to me.

I nodded, glad she didn't ask any more questions.

"What are you working on?" Sid asked, looking at Epona's papers.

"Calculating our projected harvest compared to last year's and determining if we will have enough to get us through next winter," Epona said, her brows furrowing.

I looked at her papers. They looked like scribbles to me.

Epona saw me. "Tomorrow, after dinner, you and Ludmilla will begin your lessons in writing."

I nodded affirmatively and scarfed down the rest of my dinner. Almost immediately, I began to feel drunk from the food. Sid's eyes also drifted.

"Go to bed, girls," Epona said with a laugh.

Thankful, Sid and I departed.

Outside, Sid pulled me into an embrace. Her body was a frail thing, her bones jutting out sharply from just below her skin. But she felt warm and so familiar.

"So what was your name when I was Boudicca?" I whispered in her ear.

"Aife," Sid whispered back. "But more importantly, your friend...always and forever. So, goodnight, Raven Beak," she said, tapping me playfully on the nose, then headed back toward her house.

I smiled as I watched her go then went back to my own little house. Inside, Ludmilla was already sleeping. I crawled into bed beside my puppy who now wore a small wreath, a protective amulet, around her neck. I was curious but far too exhausted to examine it. Besides, my mind felt like it was bursting. One day I was sitting, bored, at the hearth beside Madelaine. The next day my world was full of magical tidings and old, forgotten things: I was a reincarnate of the warrior queen

Boudicca, but I was called Cerridwen by the magical Wyrd Sisters who had shown me *my* King. A month before I had lamented that I couldn't do embroidery; now I was firmly in the hands of the Goddess. The thought of it filled me from head to toe with nervous passion.

nine

FOR THE NEXT FEW WEEKS, I worked with Uald in the
smithy. Since court dresses were too cumbersome, I
wore my travel breeches and cut my night dresses at the
waist as a tunic. The first few days my arms ached. As I
continued to work, however, my body got used to the
feeling. All my life I'd been kept from men's work, but
now I could see. I loved it, and so did Uald. In fact, Uald
surprised me one morning when instead of instructing
me to pound steel, she handed me a sword, but not just
any sword, a claymore.

I lifted the heavy weapon. The metal hilt felt cold in
my hands, but I liked the feel of the weapon. I'd always
wanted to learn the ways of the sword, like the warrior
queens of old, but I wasn't allowed. It was thought too
vulgar for a woman to wield a weapon. Sunlight glinted
off the blade. I swished the sword back and forth.
Boudicca. Was it true? Were the visions memory or
madness? I had always been imaginative, that was
certain, but those who followed the old ways believed a

spirit lived many lives. Yet visions sometimes spoke of madness, and my head hummed oddly when I thought of it, like I was hearing muffled voices, as if time had thrust itself out of joint. I gripped the steel and closed my eyes. I was not mad. I had remembered Boudicca's world, the feel of my body and the warmth of my blood. It was time to practice my skills again.

"I think that claymore weighs more than you do," Uald said with a grin. "Well, let's see what you've got," she added. Giving the short sword she was holding a spin, Uald stood ready.

I lifted the sword clumsily and swung it from side to side, trying to get the feel of the weapon. It was very heavy, but I loved it.

"Ready?" Uald asked.

I nodded.

"Just try to block me. Move the sword in my path."

I nodded again, and Uald made the first lunge. She was so fast that it caught me by surprise. I didn't have a chance to move in time. Moments later, I was looking at Uald down the length of her blade.

"Dead," she said, pulling her blade back. "Try again."

I grinned at her, held the sword, and waited.

Uald lunged again. My instincts worked against me. I wanted to block but my body moved clumsily. She then feinted. I tried to parry, but seconds later, her blade was resting lightly on my neck.

"Dead again," she said. "Tighten your grip, and try to feel the center of your body. Get your balance."

Again we moved. Once more I tried to block her but to no avail. On this stroke, however, a vision flashed through my mind. I saw myself on the battlefield, my wild red hair flying around me as a Roman soldier advanced. He wore a glimmering gold-colored breastplate and helmet with a red plume at the top. Like Uald, he struck, but this time I blocked...with a shield, sticking my short sword into the soldier's gut. It was so natural. I went in for the kill easily and with a spin of the sword, I turned and decapitated the Roman soldier behind me. I took off his head with one quick stroke. A waterfall of blood sprayed across the horizon following the head that spun off into the distance. The startling image rocked me from my memory.

"Cerridwen?" Uald asked, taking me by the arm. "Are you all right?"

I nodded. "Do you have a shield? And a one-handed sword?"

Uald raised an eyebrow at me then nodded. "See something?"

"Let's...well, let's just try."

Uald handed me a round buckler and short sword. I slid the shield into place and gripped the sword. Suddenly, everything felt much more familiar.

"Block," Uald commanded, then came at me, moving quickly.

This time, I tried not to think. I just moved. Moments later, I heard a clang and felt a vibrating thud when Uald's sword hit my shield.

Uald laughed out loud.

I looked to see that not only had I blocked her advance, but my sword's point was sitting an inch away from her belly.

"Well, seems we found your weapons," she said and pulled back. "Either that or you are channeling the Morrigu. Try not to kill me," Uald said with a grin.

Once more we stood at the ready. "Again," Uald called, and we began. Centuries-old memories made my arms move. I was clumsy. I needed practice, but I remembered the feel of short sword and shield in my hands.

Uald and I practiced like this every morning, clashing arms in the morning mist. It was my favorite part of the day. Slowly, I became less clumsy. My body grew stronger. My physical form molded itself into the form of a warrior woman.

While Uald kept my body busy, Epona filled my mind. Ogham, the language of the trees, and the oldest written language known to Epona, was the first language Ludmilla and I were taught. We learned how each symbol, lines with slashes, corresponded to letters and to trees. And Epona read us the ancient poem *Cad Goddeau*, "The Battle of the Trees," written by the druid Taliesin.

"There are ancient teachings buried in the poems," Epona explained, "as there are in many of the old tales. Taliesin was a great druid, and in the poem he tells how he enchanted the very trees, turning them into warriors, to fight on his side. He evokes the energy of the earth and sends an army of trees to advance on a citadel:

> *The alders in the front line*
> *began the affray.*
> *Willow and rowan-tree*
> *were tardy in array.*

The holly, dark green
Made a resolute stand;
He is armed with many spear-points
Wounding the hand.

"But was it the trees themselves, their ancient energies molded into fighting men, or was it the natural energy, the magic found from brewing leaf and root, that did the fighting? If each tree is a letter, does the battle represent a battle of wit or a battle of steel? Taliesin's poem would have us believe the woods advanced upon the castle, but such wizardry seems lost, and impossible.

"The more you study the mystery of the ancient rhymes, the more you will feel the true meaning, the true answer," Epona told us.

"What is the answer?" Ludmilla asked.

In my mind, I imagined Taliesin standing before the forest chanting long-dead languages, the trees morphing from their corporeal forms into airy figures, fighting men made of the green. Taliesin had transformed the trees into men.

Epona smiled. "I'll leave that for you to discover," she said coyly.

I loved learning about the goddess and the old ways from Epona. And very soon, it came time for Ludmilla and me to take our goddess names. After dinner one evening near Beltane, the fertility festival of spring, Druanne set two blue glass bottles on the table.

"The brew is ready," Druanne said to Epona.

She nodded affirmatively.

"What does it do?" I asked, picking up one of the bottles.

Druanne took it from me and set it back down on the table. "It will allow your Goddess to come to you, speak to you, so you can learn your Goddess name."

"Tomorrow you must eat or drink nothing. You will be given the elixir at sunset. Druanne will guide you," Epona told us.

"Oh, how exciting!" Bride said with a clap of her hands. "Shall we wager on it? Our blonde lass here looks like she belongs to a spring maid."

Ludmilla looked uncertain, nervous.

"We shall see," Epona replied simply.

I passed a glance to Sid who winked at me. At least I knew which goddess to expect.

The next day, Uald and I pulled the maypole from the barn rafters and lugged it to the center square. We bedecked the top of the pole with bright colored ribbons and a crown of flowers. Uald spent the rest of the day chopping wood and piling it near the fire rings that Druanne and Aridmis had prepared. Ludmilla, Bride, and Epona worked in Epona's house and at the fire preparing food. I strung garlands of flowers and greens, mindful to leave out snowdrops, taken from Druanne's flower garden.

I'd fasted all day. My stomach rumbled a little, but I didn't mind. I wanted to try the elixir. How would Cerridwen come to me? In a vision? In a dream? Now I would see what the Goddess wanted from me.

After the sun dropped below the horizon, Druanne came to Ludmilla and me in our little house and gave us both one of the blue bottles. "Drink, then rest on your bed. The potion will do the rest. I'll come back later to check on you both," she said then left.

Without hesitation, Ludmilla drank hers down, her face puckering at the taste.

"Well?" I asked.

"Sour," she answered and poured herself a glass of water.

I patted my little dog on her head. She had grown since we'd first come to the coven, but she still had a lot more growing to do. And she had not yet told me her name.

"Perhaps my dog should drink a little too so we can find out her name," I said with a laugh.

When Ludmilla made no sound at my jest, I looked up. She lay still on her bed. "Ludmilla?" I whispered.

She did not reply.

I laid my hand on her chest. Her heart beat slowly. "Ludmilla?"

"I hear you, sister," she said in a voice quieter than a whisper.

I looked at the flask, rolling the glass around in my hand. With a sudden surge of courage, I uncorked the top and drank. Ludmilla was right; the taste was horribly bitter. I began to feel very dizzy. I swooned.

Ludmilla rose. She stripped naked, and birds flew in the room and dressed her in a gown of gold. They laid a flower ring on her head. A golden light surrounded her. She smiled at me and disappeared in a shower of glittering dust. I looked back at her bed. Her body lay there, but her essence was missing. I scowled. I looked down at my pup.

"What's wrong?" she asked.

I stopped, disbelieving. "Ludmilla," I whispered.

"She's gone with her Goddess. Aren't you supposed to go too?" the pup asked then licked my chin. "I do like it here," she told me.

"Am I really hearing you?" I asked.

She wagged her tail.

"What is your name?"

She barked a little bark. "Why don't you call me Thora?"

I laughed. "That's a big name."

"I'll be a big dog," she answered.

I grinned, patted her on the head, and then rose. I opened the front door and looked up at the moon. It was high in the sky. The coven square was empty. The fire under the cauldron had faded; the coals glowed red. I moved through the darkness, but my feet never touched the ground. When I reached the cauldron's side, I looked in to see the moon reflected perfectly in the water, filling the oval of the cauldron with silver light. I stared into the water and a number of images rose. First I saw a white flower with five petals. It fit into the cauldron precisely, five points encapsulated by a circle. I lifted my head and looked around. The whole coven was dark. I looked into the cauldron again and saw a white sow munching on a bed of violets. I stepped back from the cauldron. A dark-robed figure stood in the shadows.

"Druanne?"

The figure took two steps toward me.

I did not move.

She dropped her hood. She had pale white skin and silver hair. Her whole body glowed. A long silver sword hung at her side. I noticed that the whole world around me glowed as she did, with silver light. All objects became black or purple, their auras silver.

I didn't breathe.

"The Goddess Cerridwen will not come to you because you are the Goddess Cerridwen," the woman said.

I trembled. "Who are you?"

"I am your mother and your protector. I will move you, Cerridwen, where you must go. You are the avenger. You are the embodiment of an army of dead men. You are a queen. You are a goddess."

"My Lady," I whispered, bowing my head, "by what name should I address you?"

"I am the Morrigu. I am Scotia. I am Cailleach. I am the third face. I am the dark face. Call me what you will. Scotia fits this face best. I have waited a long time for you to be reborn."

"What do you want from me, Lady?"

"Vengeance. Avenge me and the land. Avenge yourself upon those who wrong you. Be the blade of the Goddess. Learn what you can here, from this circle of nine, but know you will move on, and from the next place you go, you will move as well. I will take you where you need to be. I will instill you with the power you will need. All you need to do is call upon me."

"I am blessed," I whispered, amazed. Yet at the same time, my blood began to cool. An old, dead part of me rose from a cobweb-filled grave and looked out through my eyes. It was like I was merging, become one with some ancient force that had always lived alongside me, but was never part of me. I felt it rise from the yawning darkness. My body tingled. Scotia had awakened the magic in me, and I began to see what I needed to do.

"Call your power," she whispered.

I closed my eyes and summoned up the strength within me. I felt the moonlight shining down on me. I began to glow. I began to hum. My power deafened me.

"Avenge yourself," she whispered. "Punish those who have wronged your blood."

I lifted up, as if on the wings of a bird, of a raven. I could hear the thunder of my wings as they moved through the air, pulsing under the light of the moon. My heart pounded in sync. I was flying. My eyes roved the land. A path of silvery light led me to Madelaine's castle. With my raven's eyes I could see through the citadel walls. I flew around the castle, looking through the walls, searching. He was not there. I raged. My raven eyes searched. Finally, I saw him walking from the barn to the castle. I didn't think. I didn't reason. I just acted. I dove down upon Alister with wrath and felt my claws slip into him as easy as sticking one's hand into water. He screamed a blood-curdling cry. When I rose up, his soul, like a spider web, clung to my talons. Ruthlessly, I shook his being away. On the earth below me, his body lay still.

As I lifted up on my newfound wings, I peered through castle window. I saw my aunt wrapping her arm in stiff white linen while blood trickled from her cracked lip. I opened my mouth to speak to her, but all I could hear was the cry of a raven. My aunt looked out the window, wide-eyed. She ran to the casement and stared outside, watching me as I spiraled back into the night, the moon on my wings.

I flew above the land, over the forest, back to the coven. Below me, lines of silver energy wove through the land between the dark trees and over the hills. I swooped over the forest and returned to the coven, landing once more beside the cauldron. I morphed from the raven back to myself, back to the woman I had become...Corbie no more.

"Feel no guilt, Cerridwen. Avenge where vengeance calls. I mark you as my very own. Do as vengeance and magic bids," the Goddess said, and then disappeared.

Exhausted, I fell to the earth. The coals under the cauldron kept me warm until Druanne lifted me from the ground and led me back to my house.

"What did you see?" she asked.

My whole body was shaking. What had happened? Had I really killed Alister? Was I a killer? Was it all real? "A flower with five petals enclosed by the cauldron and a white sow."

Druanne grunted. "That's all? So much for our glorious Queen. When I took my name, the Merlin came to me. It seems the Goddess Cerridwen has only shown her symbols to you."

I grinned at her rudeness. "Yes, I am Cerridwen."

ten

THE NEXT DAY I EMERGED from my house, no longer Gruoch, no longer Corbie. I was Cerridwen, and I was an avenger. Alister was dead. Finally. And I had protected the one person I truly loved.

"How were your wanderings? Would you share with us?" Aridmis asked excitedly when we sat down at Epona's breakfast table that morning.

Ludmilla smiled serenely. "I travel to the most beautiful place I ever see. Two men makes a woman out of flowers. The flower girl comes to me and tells me that I was a maiden, a woman of love. She says that power through beauty and children are mine."

I smiled at her, "I saw her walk away from her body. Birds dressed her in a silken gown and put flowers in her hair."

"The flower maiden created by druids. You will be a mistress of herbs and love potions. You will bless the crops and bring love to all who surround you. Based on the visions Ludmilla described, I chose the name of King

Arthur's beautiful wife, Gwendelofar, for her," Druanne said.

Epona raised an eyebrow at Druanne. Every girl from our land knew the Arthur tales, knew that Queen Gwendelofar had strayed from King Arthur for Lancelot. Ludmilla, however, would not have known the stories and the fate Druanne had assigned her. What a nasty trick. I glared at Druanne. She pretended not to notice.

Aridmis' quick curiosity, however, was not yet sated. She looked at me. "And what did you see?" she asked eagerly.

I smiled. What could I say? I could scarcely believe what I had seen. Had the Goddess herself really spoken to me? Told me I was…a goddess reborn? Me? But I had felt the power of the raven inside me. I had flown on its black wings and tasted its power. Just thinking of it made my heart race. Maybe I should feel sorry, shocked, or remorse for what I had done, but I didn't. Madelaine was finally safe. But would these women understand if I told them? Maybe Sid would, but she was not there. She'd gone again to the barrows. And certainly, Druanne would never understand. "The sow…the star flower…and it seemed as though I traveled on raven's wings across the night's sky, under the eye of the moon. But most importantly, I learned my dog's name is Thora."

Everyone laughed.

"Clearly, she is Cerridwen, a lady of the cauldron. Knowledge and spells will be her work," Druanne said.

Bride patted my hand. "Another sister of the Great Mother's dark face. That is well."

Epona drained her cup and sat looking at the leaves therein.

"No more smithy for her," Uald said with a grin.

"I wouldn't say that," Epona said absently as she studied the leaves, but she did not elaborate.

Soon after, it was time to for our morning rites. It was Beltane, a high holy day for the order of the nine. We ate quickly and went outside.

Epona gathered us in a circle around the fire ring. Without Sid and the wandering Tully, we were only seven, but I could still feel magic resonating. We held hands as Epona called out.

"Mother, we stand here before you as seven of nine daughters. We are your children and your sisters. We worship you and call you into our midst."

All our attention then turned on the spirit of the Goddess, and it seemed to me that she was present with her earthy, wet magic. I could hear the sound of the birds. I could feel the morning dew, the damp resin of life, on my skin. The rising sun felt warm and soothing on my black hair. A soft breeze full of the fresh, green scents of spring swirled around us. It set my dress, a light blue gown with flower embroidery, aflutter.

"Mother," Epona called, "on this festival of fertility, we ask you to bless the crops. Let the spring sowing lead to a bountiful harvest. We ask for your loving help, for you to bless the wombs of maidens. May wise souls be born into this earthly plane. We ask you for peace in our land. In return, we give ourselves, your daughters, whole and complete. We dedicate our spirits to your purpose, and we dedicate our wills to heal the land."

Epona became silent, letting her words trail off into the ether. After several moments, she turned her attention to us. "What say you, sisters? For what do you ask, and what will you give in return?"

Druanne's voice sounded. "Mother, I ask you to let the land be fruitful with healing herbs so I may better serve your people. In return, I offer my services as cultivator and healer." Druanne stepped forward and threw a bundle of white sage into the flames. The smoke from the smudge filled the space. We all breathed deeply, letting the herb clear our minds.

Uald's voice rose next. "Mother, I ask for successful hunts but pray that the wildlife be repopulated. I honor the sanctity of the herds. In return, I offer the length of my hair."

Uald drew a dagger from her belt. She then cut off her long brown braid and threw it into the fire. The fire crackled. A whirlwind of ash rose upward followed by the smell of burning hair. It was a heavy sacrifice. I studied Uald's face. Her brow was furrowed. I wondered what secret wish she might have asked for.

"Mother, I come to you as the Crone," called Bride's voice. I turned to look at her. "I ask that you use me in these last few years. Make me your instrument. Don't let me sit as an old woman beside the fire. I ask for purpose. I offer you this gift, a prayer cloth embroidered by my own hands."

Bride lifted the prayer cloth so we could all see it. It was a fine thing, a long stretch of linen sewn with birds, leaves, acorns, and swirling symbols like those I had seen carved into the standing stones that dotted the lands. She had sewn words in Ogham, names of the

Goddess, and blessings. Such prayer cloths were used during childbirth and at sickbeds to protect the vulnerable. It was heavy hearth magic. Bride handed the cloth to Epona who took it gently, kissing Bride on both cheeks.

Everyone turned to Gwendelofar, who stood beside me. "Mother, I ask you guides me on my new path, and teaches me where I should go. Give me your wisdom, and, in return, I give you morning prayers."

It was a simple enough offering. Now it was my turn. My mind still reeling from my midnight ride, I took a deep breathe. "Mother, I ask that you take pity on yourself. Weep for the land. Weep for the people who have forgotten you. When your weeping is done, I ask you to take up your sword and banish the White Christ from this land. In return, I give my blood." I pulled a small dagger from my belt then sliced open the palm of my hand. I let my blood flow into the fire. It sizzled when it hit the hot coals. The smell of the burning liquid joined the smell of the sage and Uald's burnt hair. The heady scent of death and sacrifice filled the air.

The circle had stiffened and, perhaps, had taken in a breath at my call, but it was mine to make. The aching throb in my hand felt powerful. The dark spirit inside me had not left, and it smiled with satisfaction.

Aridmis broke the tension, her voice ringing like a silver bell, cutting the strange silence my vow had made. "Mother, I ask for clarity of vision so that the images before my eyes may be understood. In return, I spin the silver wheel to the future and offer this knowing: this coven will survive for six hundred more years, and when it is finally disbanded, your daughters will not be lost to you. They will carry on in new ways. You will not be forgotten." Her words settled the air my vow had stirred.

"Mother, for myself I ask that you watch over our sisters, Sid and Tully," Epona called. "Their travels take them far and to dangerous places. Protect them. In return, I offer my skills as teacher. I shall keep your coven full and fill your daughters' minds. May our words ride on the wind. May our wishes become substance. May our hearts be full. We give thanks. So mote it be."

"So mote it be," we called in reply.

Everyone smiled and began to disband. Blood dripped from my hand to the ground. Druanne came to me, pulling a piece of clean cloth from her healer's satchel. She pressed it into my hand. "Come, let's bandage this less infection set in."

She led me to the house she shared with Aridmis. The seer had large pieces of parchment spread all over the walls, mapping what I supposed were the stars. Druanne's side of the room was filled with jars and drying herbs.

"You are very different from the other women here," Druanne said as she sat me down on her bed. She frowned as she looked over her jars. Her mouth was pulled into two tight lines as she emptied a pinch of root and leaves into a mortar. I smelled a sharp scent that reminded me of anise. She ground the herbs to a find powder and mixed them with a salve.

I chose not to respond. I didn't want to go to war with her.

Druanne washed my hand and began rubbing the salve on the wound. "Druidic law teaches us to *harm none*, but it seems you feel that law does not apply to you."

I smiled and thought on Scotia's words, remembering the Goddess and what she had said to me. I would harm, but only those who deserved to be harmed. I would protect the innocent, and I would punish those who brought ill will, cruelty for meaningless gains and destruction. It was beyond what Druanne could conceive and so I was sad for her in that she was so wrong.

Druanne looked sharply at me. "I am not wrong," she told me, pulling the bandage too tight.

I inhaled deeply. "Can you hear my thoughts?" I asked through gritted teeth.

"Scant pictures," she answered. "Words as if spoken on the wind. But I heard you now, and I am not wrong. What has the Goddess said to you?"

"Why would I tell you? And what else have you stolen from my mind?"

"Just pictures. I needed to know what kind of girl you are...you are dangerous."

"What pictures? Name them," I said, not asking, but commanding.

"A man with black hair and blue eyes. You think of him often," she said as she tugged on the bandage again.

"Yes, I do," I replied. Many times my mind wandered, and I dreamed of the man the Wyrd Sisters had called my King. I puzzled it over more than I cared to admit.

"And the Wyrd Sisters. You think of them more."

I said nothing.

"They are an old and dangerous magic. Their art is not part of our world; it comes from a land now lost. They are something other, and they cannot be trusted. Their ways are not our ways. You are not one of us."

"The mind, Margaret," I said, suddenly knowing Druanne's given name, "is a trunk full of wisdoms, secrets, desires, and shames. Don't you dare judge me by what secrets you've pulled from me without my permission. I am a young woman and have not yet lived. Think of how you might hate me when you come to know my future. *Harm none* may belong in your trunk, but *protect* belongs in mine. Don't slip your fingers too deeply in or the lid may fall and break them off," I threatened.

"Or would you rather I look into your trunk?" I continued. "I see you riding away from a hovel where two children and a man slept softly, unknowingly, inside while you abandoned them. Your own children, your family, left behind…what kind of woman are *you*?" I said, my voice full of venom. I pulled my hand from her grasp.

Druanne paled.

"How does it feel to have someone draw from the well of your mind? Perhaps, all these years, when you have stolen from other people without them inviting you have been trespassing on a sacred ground. See how it feels, Margaret? Is it kindness? Is it right? No. It is harm. Despite all your pompous piousness, you are no better than the priests of the White Christ."

Druanne slid to the floor.

It was Scotia who had given me the images, given me Druanne's secrets.

"How do you know those things?" she whispered.

"It doesn't matter," I said and rose. "You are my sister. Treat me with the same respect that you ask for yourself, and we shall get along just fine," I said. Extending my good hand, I helped the tall woman to her feet.

Druanne looked shaken. "I apologize," she said, her voice quivering.

I squeezed her hand tightly, a bit too tightly. "Never again."

She shook her head. "No, never again."

I let her go. "Thank you for the mend," I said, looking at my bandaged hand.

"No, thank you," she replied absently as I turned and left her house.

I stepped outside then leaned against Druanne's door. I closed my eyes. My head thundered with the sound of raven's wings, and rage made my hands shake. My anger came too quick, too ready. I took a deep breath and quieted the raven inside me.

eleven

A PARTY OF FIVE MEN RODE into the coven. Their rough and brawny appearance made it seem as though we were being invaded by Vikings. But they were the bards of the north, handsome men more built for warfare than music. Each man carried an instrument strapped to his back; some carried a battle axe or a sword as well.

Epona rushed to greet them while Uald helped with their horses.

"Cerridwen?" Epona called.

I crossed the yard to join her.

"This is Bergen," Epona said, introducing me to a fair-haired giant with a harp strapped across his back, "He is the chief bard amongst this group." Bergen's long locks were braided at the temples. He also wore braids in his beard. He had swirling tattoos around his forehead and down his arms.

"My Lord," I said with a curtsey.

"My my, a Lady amongst your flock, Epona?" he said with a smile.

She smiled in reply but said nothing.

Gwendelofar joined us. "He-hello," she stammered meekly.

Bergen smiled at her. "Good morrow to you, Mistress. Men, where are your manners? Come meet Epona's new sisters," he called to the others, introducing us to Brant, Ivar, Frey, and Sigurd in turn.

The bards bowed to us.

"Ladies, we shall have music tonight!" Brant, a dark haired bard with a beard that stretched to his belly said as he strummed his lute. "Praise be to the gods!"

The bard introduced as Sigurd, a tall man with fiery red hair and deep blue eyes, laughed. "If you're not passed out by nightfall!" He then smiled toward Uald and leaned in toward Gwendelofar and me, "I'd recite you fine ladies a romantic ballad, but Uald finds them dull," he said teasingly.

"Love poetry *is* dull," Uald replied, just barely hiding her smile, then headed off to the barn with the horses. "Sing about battle," she called with a laugh.

"Are you sure she isn't a raven goddess?" Frey, who had a drum strapped on his back, asked Epona.

It was my turn to laugh.

"Perhaps these ladies are more romantically-minded?" Ivar, a slim man whose bald head was covered in tattoos, said to Gwendelofar and me.

Gwendelofar smiled kindly at Ivar then turned to Sigurd. "I would like to hear,'" she said but blushed and looked down, her long lashes resting on her cheeks. Beltane was truly the holiday for maidens. Gwendelofar looked lovelier than ever, her skin was pale but her cheeks were as rosy as apples.

"You see, there is always one romantic in the crowd," Sigurd yelled to Uald who waved dismissively, shaking her head. "Of course, My Lady, as you wish" he told Gwendelofar.

I grinned at them.

"Come," Epona called. She led everyone to the benches around the fire and soon Brant and Bergen were playing a tune. Aridmis and Druanne, who wouldn't meet my eye, joined us. Aridmis began pouring ale and honey mead for our guest. The sounds of the lute and harp chimed through the forest in harmony.

I headed to the stables to help Uald.

"Lend you a hand?" I called.

"Well, that sliced one will be no good to me for a day or so, but I'll take the other," she replied with a laugh. "I've just filled the water trough. Mind leading them over?"

Taking the reins of the bards' horses, I led the motley crew to the water. They drank quickly while they whinnied back and forth with the mares in the pen. Kelpie was not pleased about the competition. He neighed loudly and kicked at the fence in outrage. After all, he'd just become king of his little herd.

Uald laughed. "Bunch of horney lads, just like those men over there. They *are* good men, Corb-Cerridwen, but they are men all the same," she said as she came to stand beside me, watching the horses drink. Uald leaned against the barn wall, gazed at the bards, then leaned in close to me. "Epona won't say a word, but Elaine would probably curse me if I didn't remind you that *your* maidenhead comes with a price…set by the King. Here we are free, but I know it's not the same for you as it wasn't with Elaine. But your life is your own. Choose your own path."

I nodded. I knew her words were true. I had to enter whatever bridal contract was drawn up for me as a maiden. When the Great Mother had ruled the land, women had ruled their wombs, but today this was not so. I felt indignant. If I chanced upon a man I wanted, I would let no such rules stop me.

"You know, I saw you once when you were just a little girl," Uald continued. "Elaine met me at the brook to show you to me. What a darling thing you were, pretty raven-headed child. She loved you so much. You were wicked though. You damned near drowned just trying to splash her. Boite's daughter. A wild little pixie." She paused and looked at me. "Ah, what the hell, come on, let's go get drunk," she said with a laugh. Taking me by the arm, Uald led me across the yard and filled us tankards of ale. We sat down by the fire and drank.

Soon Aridmis joined the men in song. They began to recite the tale of Emer and Cú Chulainn. I cast a glance around the circle. Emer. It had been my mother's name. How odd she would find me there.

I knew the story well. In my mind, it had become one with the tale of my own father and mother:

> *In the land of Ulster across the sea*
> *The Lady Emer possessed great beauty*
> *Adored by the hero Cú Chulainn*
> *Emer would wife this man of legend*

Forgall sent brave Cú Chulainn to Alba
To Skye and the lady of Shadows
Mighty Cú Chulainn would prove his prowess
If he would win the fair Emer
Sword, shield, and axe did the Lady teach
But still Forgall denied Cú Chulainn's reach
So brave Cú Chulainn wrung Emer from her father's side
To wed her and bed her and make her a bride
Fair Emer, whose love never faltered
And Cú Chulainn whose love never died
Forever they live in the land of the young
In bliss

Aridmis' voice was sweet and rung like a bell. Her words echoed across the hills. The legend of Emer soaked into the land, and I wondered, not for the first time, about my family across the sea. To my Irish family, I was nothing more than a bastard. But whose bastard was I? On what throne on the Isle of the Mighty did my maternal grandfather sit? Whose Eerie blood ran in my veins? All my life I was told, and I knew from my father, that I was the kin of Kenneth MacAlpin, the great hero of Alba, the man who had quelled the Picts, united the clans, a High King of Scotland. I was a MacAlpin. But to what other family did I belong? Why did no one ever speak of it? Maybe, my mother and father both gone, no one knew anymore. The thought saddened me.

Between playing songs, the men talked of their travels and gave us news of the outside world. Through them I learned that King Malcolm was busy fighting King Magnus of Norway from his shores and was at odds with Lord Thorfinn over the ownership of the northern-most provinces of Scotland. To the south, English King Cnut was fighting amongst his own people and lesser lords who had risen against him. Unsurprisingly, the affairs of men were the same as always.

Bride poured ale for the men and laughed as they flirted teasingly with her.

"You lads would be surprised," she told them. "I am, after all, named Bride. Why do you think they gave the name of the loveliest maidens to me? When I was their age," she said, motioning to Gwendelofar and me, "you would have lined up to woe me."

"I'll still form a line!" Brant exclaimed.

"Can you even see your cock over that belly?" Bride asked, causing everyone to burst out laughing, Bergen spitting his ale out his nose.

The day wore on and by the time the second party of men arrived, everyone was quite drunk, myself included.

"One of the last bands of Druids," Aridmis said when Epona went to greet them.

I raised an eyebrow at her. "One of?"

"There are more...small, secret groups. Their order is all but done, but when they can, they still guide kings...and queens," she said, casting a glance at me.

I watched them dismount, my eyes resting on the youngest of them, a man maybe five years older than myself. He was tall, nicely built, and his brownish-red hair simmered in the light of the fire. Moments later I found myself on my feet, joining Epona to meet them. I felt almost like some force had snared me and pulled me—to him.

"Ah, Cerridwen, this is Balor. He is an Arch Druid," Epona introduced. Balor was a thin, bald-headed man who wore long gray robes. His eyes matched their stormy color.

Balor looked closely at me. "My Lady," he said with sincerity.

I understood then that he knew who I was, who I really was, but I knew my secret would be safe with such a man. I had never been in the presence of an Arch Druid before. The enormity of his title struck me deeply. "An honor," I said.

Balor nodded kindly toward me.

"These are Balor's students. Calean, I know," Epona said, introducing me to a young man with long, straight black hair. She turned to the young, handsome druid. "And Lord Banquo, isn't it?" Epona asked.

"I'll leave the titles to my father. Here, I'm just a servant of the ancient ones," Banquo said, motioning to the small tattoo of a stag's head on his brow. Such designs were frowned upon by the priests of the White Christ, but the worshippers of the old ways would know the symbol. A man could only receive the mark of the stag after being initiated in the rites of Cernunnos, the Lord of the Forest. "Just Banquo, please," he told Epona, but I couldn't help but notice that his eyes were on me.

I smiled at him as I eyed him over. His muscular arms were tattooed with the swirling Pictish designs of animals, trees, leaves, and birds. Banquo's skin was tanned from hours in the sun. His brown hair, touched lightly with red, curled softly around his face. He was the most handsome man I had even seen...save, perhaps, the black-haired man in my visions.

Banquo's dark eyes met mine. He winked playfully at me.

I looked away, surprised to feel my cheeks redden.

"Cerridwen, perhaps Banquo would like some wine?" Epona suggested then left us, escorting Balor and Calean to the other side of the fire.

"Please," I said to Banquo, motioning to a bench nearby. I turned, reached for the jug of wine, but felt Banquo's hand on mine.

"Please, My Lady, allow me," he said, taking the bottle from my hand. "I hope you take no offense, but my mother would never forgive me if I let a daughter of the goddess serve me."

"Your mother is very wise," I said with a nervous laugh. My hands shook. I felt like a fool.

"So…Cerridwen?" Banquo asked as he handed me the drink. "Named for the Welsh cauldron goddess?" I noticed then that he had stags' heads tattooed on his hands as well, the antlers extended out onto his fingers. He must have participated in heavy earth magic to earn such marks.

"Cerridwen, yes, amongst other names," I said with a sly grin. I realized my voice was slurring somewhat.

"Ah, yes, Cerridwen would be your goddess name. Now," he said, leaning in toward me as he sipped his wine, "tell me why you look so familiar. Have we met before?"

I looked closely at him. His eyes were dark brown, the color of acorns in fall. He had a strong, square jaw and just the hint of a beard. He was so striking. I would remember such a fine man visiting Alister's estate, but no man so lovely had ever graced those halls. And yet, I recognized him. The ale and the magic of Beltane had my mind lost in a haze. "No, we haven't, but you look familiar to me too," I told him. My stomach fluttered.

Banquo smiled, his cheeks dimpling. "Perhaps... Inverness?"

I shook my head. "I've never been there."

"Maybe we were friends in another life," Banquo said and took my hands. "Let me see. Your callouses are new, your fingernails are unbroken, such lovely, soft, sweet hands. Are you from a royal house?"

"Aren't you, Lord Banquo?" I smiled at him and squeezed his hands.

"I suppose I am," he said with a laugh.

"Do you suppose that's why Epona left us alone?" I said in a mock-suspicious whisper.

"Shall we talk affairs of state?" he asked with a sarcastic deepening of his voice. "Which successor do you favor, Lady? Duncan, Thorfinn, or Macbeth? Or do you promote Moray? Shall we plot the line of succession or shall we discuss the life in service of spirit? Which do you prefer?" He paused. His voice calmed. "Let's start with how you find this life?"

His boldness surprised me. It caught me off guard to hear my cousins' names bandied about so freely. Banquo didn't know who I was, how important the next successor was to the course of my life. The thought that, in this place, it mattered so little, amused me. I chuckled. "Let the Wyrds sort out the kingdom. The castle was a prison. This life is far more preferable."

Banquo lifted his cup. "I'll drink to that," he said, taking a swallow. He gazed into his cup. "The castle life...I agree, a prison...a brothel...or worse. My father liked his whores more than his children. The castle is no place for me either."

"How terrible for you."

"It's worse for my mother," he said with a frown. His soft features hardened a bit, and I saw the pain behind his eyes.

"I'm sorry...for you and your mother. In the very least, it is a blessing you have her," I said, the sting of the poem of Emer and Cú Chulainn still fresh.

He smiled softly at me. "You lost your mother?"

"In childbed."

"She must have been very beautiful, though. You are quite stunning. Are your eyes purple? I've never seen violet eyes before."

"My looks come from my father. My mother was fair."

"And your father, is he—"

"Dead as well."

I realized then that Banquo was still holding my hands. He gently stoked my fingers, my knuckles. He looked deeply into my eyes. "You're an orphan," he said gently.

Surely, I was drunk. I fell silent and started to weep. Somehow, this man, this newcomer had brought up all my hurt and anger at the loss of my parents. Maybe it was the ballad of Emer and Cú Chulainn. Or maybe it was Beltane, or maybe the ale, or maybe it was just...him. My parents, their loss was a deep sorrow I rarely touched, and here it had been uprooted.

He wiped a tear off my cheek. "I'm an idiot. I'm sorry. I didn't mean...I just opened my mouth and...the words just came tumbling out. I'm sorry."

"No. It's not you," I whispered. "It's the drink," I said, trying to chuckle.

"Balor is like a father to me," he said, his gaze going to Balor and Epona. Calean had moved off and was chatting with Druanne. Poor man. Balor and Epona were sitting very close to one another, talking in low tones. But Epona was smiling in a way I'd never seen her smile before. I realized then that she was flirting. I was surprised.

"He and Epona are...familiar," I commented.

"By the end of the night, I'd wager they will be very familiar," Banquo said with a grin.

I giggled, wiping the tears away.

"How old is she, I wonder?" Banquo asked.

"Her face tells one tale, her hair another."

"They say that those who have done grim magic sometimes loose the pigment in their hair, the magic draining them, but she seems very kind."

I gazed at Epona, wondering what arts she might have worked that would have changed her so. "She is."

"It's good that you are with her."

The tears welled again, but I fought them back. "Have you any siblings?" I asked.

"A sister who died during the harsh winter two years ago," he said sadly. "And you?"

"Two half-brothers who did not outlive their cradles," I said. My father had taken a second wife, but she had produced no surviving heirs, and like my mother, had died trying. It made me terribly sad to think of it. "Let's talk of happier things. What does Balor teach you, if I may ask?"

"To read, write, heal, and...well...other things."

"Other things...now, that's the interesting part."

Banquo smiled at me again, once more evoking his dimples.

"Do those 'other things' include your tattoos?" I asked, reaching up to just barely stroke the tattoo on his forehead. When I did, I felt a sudden jolt. My whole body shook and for a brief moment, I was caught up in a vision. I saw and felt Banquo and I in bed together, naked, making love. In my vision, my long red hair fell in a wild tumble around me. Banquo's hair was also red and was pulled back in a long braid that tickled my nipples as he thrust into me, his hot mouth on mine. But the eyes, his eyes were still the same chestnut color. I gasped.

Banquo quickly grabbed my hand and peered deeply at me. He'd gone pale.

"Did you...did you see?" I stammered.

Banquo nodded. "Heady magic," he said, leaning in, away from the bards. "There are old places where the world is thin. Old places," Banquo whispered, "where old souls remember. Balor says this coven is special, that it is a place of heavy magic. The forgotten world lives just beyond," he said, motioning to the dark woods around us. "I made my voyage and came back full of old knowing. I feel that same energy here. Soul magic," he whispered, looking down at my hand. He wore an odd expression on his face.

"I know the places you speak of," I replied in a whisper. Truly, the barrow where Sid had taken me was a place of heavy magic. But I had journeyed there and elsewhere through the thin veil between the worlds to the Wyrd Sisters. And where, exactly, was it that I had found them? Where did they reside? I didn't know. I wondered if Banquo had seen them as well? Would it be a betrayal to ask him? I wasn't sure. I looked at Banquo. The symbols he wore were men's magic, the craft of the horned god, not the Wyrd Sisters. But what of soul magic? It was often said that when two old souls who have lived many lives came together once again, they remembered each other. That was what Banquo meant. Our shared vision…it had been soul magic.

"Banquo…" I began but a movement caught my eye. Gwendelofar and Sigurd rose and went into the cabin we shared. The others noticed as well, but no one said a word, not even Brant. A moment later, Thora came padding out, looking as if she'd just been awoken from a nap. Confused, she paused and looked around at all the newcomers.

"Here," I called. I gazed at Banquo but said nothing else.

Thora scampered happily toward me.

"This is Thora," I said, scratching her head when she joined us.

She began attacking Banquo's boot laces.

"Thora, eh?" He ruffled her ears. Thora cut the odd energy between us, the nervous familiarity. Soul magic.

Thora nipped playfully at him.

"Vicious little monster," he said teasingly, "I bet she can track though, can't you, you little wild thing?" he asked Thora, playing with her. Thora chewed on his shirt cuff and tried to nip hands. She was loving every minute of it.

"Is tracking difficult to train?" I asked.

Banquo shook his head. "Give her the scent of something then go hide it. She will learn to find it, won't you? Little bad girl. Why did you name her Thora?"

I shrugged. "I didn't. She told me her name."

"How?"

"I think that goes into the 'other things' category."

Banquo laughed then smiled at me. I stared into his soft brown eyes. My whole body felt alive, tingling. Something about this man sparked an inner fire in me. If felt light, giddy, near him. It was the first time I'd ever experience such a feeling before.

Banquo was right about Epona and Balor. After the moon had risen to its zenith, they disappeared into the woods. Uald, who had been drinking great quantities of ale, passed out by the fire. Druanne and the Druid Calean were still deep in talk when Aridmis and Bride went to bed. I sighed, figuring Gwendelofar would not be out of the house again until morning. The bards had spread out their blankets and slept by the fire.

By the end of the night, if not before, I was drunk. The world around me blurred, and the passage of time slowed considerably.

"It seems you've lost your bed," Banquo said.

I nodded.

"You can share my mat, if you will. No harm will come to you. The Mother knows, you are the loveliest creature to ever step foot on this green earth, but I swear to keep my hands to myself," Banquo offered.

"Only if there is room for Thora," I said with a grin, but my stomach was full of butterflies. Did I dare lie down with a handsome stranger? *Was* he really a stranger?

I watched as Banquo spread out his blankets by the fire. He lay down then held out his hand to me. Nervously, I lay down beside him. He gently curled his arms around me. How loving it felt. He smelled of musk and mint. It was a sweet, manly smell. And it smelled so familiar. His body was warm, the blankets soft. I could feel the curves of his muscular arms. I looked up at the stars overhead and exhaled deeply while Thora made a bed at our feet. For a moment, I felt something I'd never felt for a man before. It felt a little like love.

twelve

T HE REVELRY OF BELTANE EVE would continue on to
further revelry on Beltane day. I woke, however,
with my head pounding, a sour taste in my mouth, and
my head lying on Banquo's chest. It was early morning
still; the sun had barely risen. I closed my eyes and
soaked up his warmth. I surprised myself. It felt so good
to be close to him.

I opened my eyes again to see Epona, Druanne, and
Aridmis setting food out on the breakfast table. The
sweet scent of fresh baked bread filled the air. Bride was
sitting by the fire turning sweet cakes over on the
cooking stone. She winked at me. My cheeks reddened.
It wasn't like that. Nearby, Uald snored loudly.
Untangling myself carefully from Banquo, I rose
quietly. He stirred but slept on. I covered him then
headed to my house.

I entered quietly. I hoped Sigurd and Gwendelofar
would still be asleep. I didn't want to interrupt their
intimate time. My wish was granted. They were both

sleeping. I moved silently so not to wake them. Gwendelofar was covered by her soft coverlet, but Sigurd lay uncovered and stretched out on the bed beside her. He was a hulking figure and naked as a babe. I saw he had tattoos all across his chest and down his waist, the tattoos stopping just above his sleeping cock nestled on a bed of straw-colored hair. I paused, feeling my heart beating harder. For a moment I imagined what it would be like to bed him, to feel him inside me, but his image got tangled up in my imagination with Banquo. Gwendelofar stirred and turned, uncovering her breasts. Her small pink nipples were erect in the morning air. She looked so beautiful. I wondered for a moment what it would be like to join them in that bed, to feel both of their naked skin against mine: his cock and her soft, sweet breasts. My cheeks reddened. I turned away from them, knowing the energy of Beltane was getting the better of me. I grabbed a clean dress from my trunk and headed back outside.

Beside the fire, Banquo still slept. Thora had taken my spot on the mat beside him, no doubt soaking up the last of my warmth. I followed the small trail behind the coven to the deep pool at the spring. I removed all my garments and jumped into the water. It was far colder than I expected, but the nipping chill felt wonderful. I was dipping my hair into the water when a huge wave splashed my face. The massive spray came as someone jumped into the spring. Surprised, I wiped the water from my eyes and looked around to find Sid grinning at me.

I laughed and splashed her. "Back again! And just in time. I didn't think we'd see you so soon."

"And now you've seen me right down to My Lady," she said with a naughty laugh. She bounced around in the water, washing the dirt from her face.

"Where were you?"

"It's Beltane for the Fair Ones too," Sid said with a wink but then frowned. "I need to be clean. Hush," she called to the invisible apparition above her. "Do they call you Cerridwen now?"

"Yes, and Ludmilla has become Gwendelofar."

Sid grinned wildly and dove under water. Jerking on my legs, she pulled me under. Laughing and spitting out water, I clambered back upward.

"I am glad you're back," I said, "I think."

She laughed. "Are the men here?"

I nodded. "Epona and the others are preparing breakfast for them now."

"Ah, Epona the pleaser. Do you know she is over eighty years old?"

"She cannot be."

"Glamour," Sid said simply and scrubbed her dirty arms.

Just then, Thora appeared at the side of the creek. She barked a little bark and looked behind her.

"I told you she could track," I heard Banquo call as he neared the side of the stream. Seeing both me and Sid naked, he then exclaimed. "Oh! I'm sorry, ladies." He turned his back.

"Don't be sorry. Strip and come in. The water is warm," Sid told him.

Grinning, I pinched her under the water.

"Cerridwen?" he queried, looking over his shoulder.

Sid brought out the wicked in me. "Yes, come join us, Banquo," I said. "Meet my sister, Sid."

He laughed nervously. "Are you sure?"

Laughing, I splashed him. He chuckled then began to undress.

"Is he yours already, Raven Beak?" Sid whispered but then got distracted by the invisible Nadia near her shoulder. "Hush! I'm asking her—"

I thought on the result of an answer in either direction and decided not to reply.

Sid smiled.

Banquo stripped down and a moment later, before I could get a good look at him, jumped into the water.

"Ahh," he yelled as the cold water hit him. "You lie, sisters."

Sid and I both laughed, but Sid swam over to him and wrapped her arms around him. "I just wanted to see you naked," she told him then looked deeply at his face. "You've the eyes of a king," she whispered.

He grinned at Sid.

"What is it you say?" Sid asked Nadia. "Ah, the eyes of a queen as well. He's beautiful, isn't he?" Sid asked me.

"Yes." He really was beautiful. And for a moment, I saw both Banquo and Sid before me with that strange double-vision as I had seen in the barrow. Once more Sid's face changed, and I saw her as Boudicca had seen her, with her pale golden hair. And I saw Banquo too. He looked as he had in the vision I'd seen the night before, his long red hair pulled back into a braid. *Prasutagus* a voice whispered from my memory. *He was Prasutagus, your husband.*

My husband, but not my King, and not the raven-haired man from my visions.

Sid stroked her hand across Banquo's chest then leaned in and kissed him while she moved his hands to her breasts.

Banquo quivered.

I giggled nervously, but for some reason, I didn't feel jealous. It felt...okay...for Sid to be there with us.

"Don't laugh, come," Sid said and pulled my hand.

I glided easily in the water.

She moved one of his hands to my breast as she kissed his neck. "Eyes of a king," she whispered in his ear.

Banquo stared at me, uncertain if he should take his hand away or not. Sensing his uncertainty, Sid pulled away from Banquo then guided me in front of him, putting his other hand on my other breast. I inhaled sharply. It felt so wonderful to have him touch me. My hands drifted to his waist. I touched his bare skin, felt his body. A feeling like lightning shot through me. Sid swam around behind me and joined her hands with Banquo's. They both gently touched my breasts, playing with my nipples. Sid then took her hands away and stuck them under the water. I shifted, uncertain, when her hands drifted between my legs. She gently moved my legs apart and touched the soft folds therein.

"So sweet," Sid whispered. "Feel," she then told Banquo. Taking one of his hands, she guided him between my legs. He gently stroked me, his fingers never intruding, just touching me gently, his thumb working the sweet spot. My whole body shook. I closed my eyes. I could feel Sid's hands on my breasts again, stroking me softly, then the feel of her wet, hot mouth sucking my nipples. Banquo leaned forward and kissed my neck as he rubbed me, touching all of me. I trembled when I climaxed.

Banquo took his hands away then held me gently by the back of my head and leaned in and kissed me. I didn't resist him. His mouth tasted sweet. I caught the light doughy taste of sweet cakes and spring water in his mouth. After a moment, he pulled back. He was breathing hard.

Sid reached up, cradled his face, and kissed him playfully. Her hands roved under the water once again, but this time she found Banquo. "Impregnate Anwyn," she whispered to him, "offer the spring your seed."

Banquo closed his eyes. He breathed deeply, and his face began to twitch with excited sensations as Sid touched him under the water. I kissed him passionately, my tongue roving inside his sweet mouth. I felt him shaking. A few moments later, he contorted with excited release. Panting, he wrapped his arms around us both and kissed our cheeks.

"You are very sweet," Sid told Banquo as she waded out of the water. Grabbing her heap of clothing, she tucked it under her arm then headed naked back to the coven, leaving me in Banquo's arms.

Banquo sat down on a large rock underwater, and I crawled onto his lap, my arms around his neck, my head resting upon his chest. I could feel his declining manhood under me. We relaxed in the cold water, Banquo's arms wrapped around me.

"What is she?" he whispered.

"A faerie thing," I replied.

"How is it I feel so deeply for you but only just met you?" he whispered.

I smiled and looked deep into his eyes. *Prasutagus.* The named floated on the wind. "This is an old love renewed," I whispered.

"May the Goddess let it be so," Banquo replied.

thirteen

THAT MORNING, WHEN THE BARDS played, the rest of us danced around the maypole. Taking hold of bright, colorful ribbons, we ladies and our druids guests wove around the tall pole and sang the songs of spring. I giggled happily as we strung the symbol of the Forest Lord, the erect maypole, with his lady's purse, the colorful ribbons. I was holding a bright purple ribbon, weaving it in and out between the other colors. Laughing, my heart pounding, I soon began to feel a little dizzy. As I danced, my mind went back in time, and I saw Madelaine threading purple thread in and out of her embroidery frame.

"How do you get it to look so perfect?" I had asked her.

I had been sitting at her side, all of the women around the house gathered by the fire sewing as the chill of deep winter blasted the castle walls.

"I don't think about it," she replied. "My hands move, do the work, but my mind is elsewhere."

"Where?"

Madelaine laughed. "That, Little Corbie, is none of your business," she said then playfully tapped my nose with one finger.

The other women giggled.

I sighed heavily then set down my sewing. "I'll be back in a minute," I said but both Madelaine and I knew it was a lie.

"Of course. Fly back soon."

I rushed out of the hall and upstairs, stopping in my chamber to grab my heavy bear-fur coat, and headed toward the castle turret. Eager to get outside and away from the boredom, I rushed as quietly as I could down the dark castle hallways toward the turret door. The brass pull on the door was freezing cold; it burned my fingers. When I opened the door, freezing wind blasted down the spiral stairwell. I went into the turret, clapping the door shut behind me, then rounded up the spiral stairs and pushed open the outer door. I emerged onto the roof, startling a flock of ravens roosting under the arches. They cawed then flew off, black specks against a white canvas. The wind whipped violently, but it was a magical sight. The whole countryside was covered in a blanket of snow that shimmered like blown diamond dust. The sun was just beginning to set. Dim hues of heather purple and marigold orange trimmed horizon.

The vista was so bleak that it surprised me when I spotted a woman standing at the top of a hill close to the castle. She wore long, flowing green robes and had golden hair the color of daffodils. I gasped when I saw her. Surely she was near freezing dressed in such a sheer gown. Her hair whipped wildly around her. A moment later, she beckoned. My skin turned to goose bumps, and I felt a sinking feeling inside as I peered more closely at her. I looked around. There was no one on the turret nor in the yard below. I gazed back at the blonde-haired woman. She beckoned once more then walked over the rise and out of sight.

Gathering up my skirts, I headed inside, snuck down the hallways and the grand staircase, and ran out the front gate. The snow was deep. I hadn't taken more than ten steps, however, when someone called my name.

"Corbie?" I turned to see Tavis, who was new to our household then, at the gate. He'd just come back from riding. His horse's winter coat, its hair long, was covered with small balls of ice. "Where are you going?"

"I..." What would I say? "I saw a woman on the hill."

"A woman? Out in this weather? Are you certain?"

I nodded vigorously. "I swear it. I was on the turret. I saw her from there. She is wearing green robes."

"Which direction?"

I pointed to the hill where I had seen the golden-haired woman.

Tavis leant me his hand then pulled me on horseback in front of him. "And just what were you doing on the turret?" he asked with a chuckle as we rode off in the direction of the hill.

"Avoiding needlework?"

Tavis laughed. "Just like your lovely aunt, always up to mischief."

Tavis' horse fought through the heavy snow. The wind blew icy cold across the hill. My nose froze, turning red. I pulled my arms inside my coat and wrapped them around me.

"Bitter cold. A person would freeze outside tonight once the sun goes down," Tavis said as we neared the hill. He road to the top, but there was no sign of the woman anywhere.

Puzzled, I looked around. "Where did she go?"

Tavis scanned the ground. "No footprints."

"Wind must have blown them awa—" I was beginning to say when I saw the woman again. She was walking over a small rise near the loch in the valley below. Her green robes and yellow hair still blew around her. She stopped and beckoned to me.

"There! There she is!" I said to Tavis, pointing excitedly toward the woman.

He peered in the distance. "Where?"

"Near the loch."

"Near the loch? I only see trees."

Again, the woman passed over the hill and disappeared.

"There, she just passed the rise. She must be lost. Hurry before it gets dark."

Tavis reined his horse in, and we fought the deep snow. The castle was lost behind us in the gusting wind. We couldn't even see our path back.

"Corbie, are you certain?" Tavis asked again. "There is nothing in this direction for twenty leagues. Why would a woman be out here?"

"I don't know, but she was just there. I swear."

We rode through the snow, finally reaching the rise where the woman had gone. We reached the pinnacle just as the sun dropped below the horizon. I scanned the frozen wasteland around us. The woman was nowhere to be seen.

"Corbie?"

I looked all around. Surely she was there. I scanned the vista. For a brief moment, I thought I saw the woman. She appeared as a shimmer on the distant horizon. I squinted to look closer. When I did, however, the woman disappeared, and I saw five black dots against the white snow, barely visible in the whipping wind.

"There, do you see that?" I asked, pointing.

Tavis following my gaze. He held his hand to his brow and gazed off into the distance. "Men," he said then.

"Who? Alister's men?"

The small party moved toward us. In the fading sunlight, amongst the party, I saw a flash of color.

Tavis clicked to his horse and headed in the direction of the party. "Did you see? Did you see that too?" he quizzed me, his voice quivering with excitement.

How could I miss it? The party rode carrying a standard boasting a black raven winging across an amethyst background. It was the standard of Boite. My father had come.

We crossed the snow quickly and soon we met with the other party. My father road with four other men, a young one of whom appeared to be injured. Boite was bent in the snow wrapping one of his men's forearm. He hadn't yet recognized me, but I could never mistake him, even though I had not seen him for at least two years. He looked enormous under the weight of his heavy furs. His head was covered by a wolf pelt, the face of the wolf hovering on his forehead.

"Hail, Your Lordship," Tavis called as he neared them.

"Are we near the castle of Lord Alister?" one of my father's men called.

My father gave us a quick, passing glance as he worked at the boy's arm, setting it in a sling.

"Yes, My Lord. I am the castle sentinel. The castle is but a league behind us."

"Good," my father said as he finished then helped the boy up and back on his horse. "We got turned around in this accursed weather. The damned horse spooked and tossed my standard bearer. His arm might well be broken. I need to get him to sist—" Boite was saying when he finally turned and looked at Tavis and me.

Finally, he rested his pale, violet-colored eyes on me. "Gruoch?"

"Father," I said with a smile, trying to hide my excitement.

My father moved quickly across the deep snow, the drift reaching up to his knees, toward me. It almost seemed as if the snow moved to make way for him. He pulled me from Tavis' horse and cradled me in his arms, pressing me tightly against his chest. When he finally relaxed his arms, he looked down at me, studied my face closely, then kissed me on my forehead. "By the Gods, what brings you out in this weather?"

I didn't know what to say. Should I tell him I'd followed a phantom woman? "Why, the Gods, of course."

Boite laughed. The sound of his voice echoed through the valley. "Then praise be to the Gods, because we were lost, my young man here is hurt, and night is upon us. Not to mention, I brought you a gift," my father said, motioning to a black horse tethered to his own steed: Kelpie. "I think you might have saved your daddy's life," he told me then kissed me on the forehead.

My father set me on his horse then turned and helped his wounded man mount. Once the man was secure, Boite swung up behind me. "Lead on, good man," he told Tavis.

Motioning to his men to follow, my father fell in behind Tavis, and we headed back through the deep snow and gusting wind toward the castle. I loved the feel of my father. He held me with one arm around my stomach, holding the reins with his other gloved hand. His black beard was grown long and was full of small balls of ice and snow. He wore heavy skins and wool clothes. His horse snorted in the cold wind, steam curling from its nostrils. The temperature was dropping fast now that the sun had set. It had grown very cold. I shivered in my gown under my heavy cloak.

"Well, Little Raven," he whispered in my ear. His voice was deep and gruff but not unkind. "Now tell me, how *did* you find us?"

Something told me he already knew. "I saw a woman."

"A woman? What did she look like, my little fledging?"

"Yellow hair the color of daffodils and long green robes."

"So you see her too?"

"I did see the woman…but I never saw her before. Not until today."

"What would you say if I told you I was following her myself? We were lost in this damned storm. When the wind gusted, we couldn't see a thing and have been riding blind. I've been following her for the last hour."

"Who is she? A faerie woman? A spirit?"

"No, lass," he said then laughed. "That was your mother."

"My…my mother?"

"Her shade, at least. I see her from time to time. She often appears when I need her. Your mother was such a lovely thing. I know the story goes that I stole Emer from her father and forced her to be my bride. But the truth is, when the castle was sacked, Emer's father brought his seven daughters before me and allowed me to choose my bride. I chose your mother for three reasons: she was the only one amongst her sisters who looked me in straight in the eyes, because she wore tattoos on her hands, marks of the old gods of the Isle of the Mighty, and because my soul knew her spirit. Soul magic. It was not the first time I'd met her spirit; I was drawn to her by a powerful force. And your mother, she knew it too. She knew the old ways and had no fear. I loved that girl for all the months she was my wife. And even before I had married her proper, I took her to the woods, and we shared vows under an ancient oak. Neither of us knew the other's language, but our souls knew one another. I hand-fasted to her before the Gods, and she was my bride. Your mother died too young, all that magic still bottled up inside her. Now you've the spark in you, Little Raven. What will you do with all that magic?"

THE RIBBON FINALLY WOUND TO the bottom of the pole, I crashed breathless onto the ground, the others laughing and giggling. Aridmis took Epona's arm and swung her in a circle as the bards played on. Even Druanne smiled, and she relaxed, breathless, onto grass. Calean, Banquo's druid companion, was twisting Sid in wide pirouettes, dancing to the music. Sid was laughing and flirting shamelessly. Banquo flopped down into the grass beside me. He put his arms behind his back and was breathing hard from dancing. After a few moments I stood up and extended my hand to him.

"Come on," I said.

He took my hand, and we headed into the woods. "Well, my lovely priestess, where are you leading me?"

"I want you to see something. I want to see if you…well, I just want you to see something," I said.

I retraced the path of nine oaks to the mound where Sid had taken me, to Boudicca's mound. The new, green leaves were shimmering overhead. Sweet young ferns, their chartreuse fingers uncurling, dotted the forest floor. The air smelled loamy under the rays of the warm spring sun. We entered the moss-covered valley where the mound sat at its center. Banquo slowed to a stop and stared at the mound. When I looked back at him, he'd gone absolutely pale.

"What...what is this place?" he asked.

I didn't say anything.

Banquo took a few steps toward the mound, staring at it, and looked back at me. He looked shocked. "Cerridwen?" he said, his voice sounding hollow. He took a step toward me and reached out and took my hand. With his other hand, he reached out and stroked a stay hair away from my face. "Your hair was red," he whispered.

I smiled up at him. "So was yours," I replied.

I cast a glance toward the burial mound. Prasutagus, Boudicca's husband, died many years before his wife. He would not have seen her burial mound. He would not have been buried nearby. But the energy of the place, the power emanating from the great queen's very bones, charged the place with memory. I wanted to see if it would affect Banquo as it had me. I wanted to see if the name whispered on the wind—Prasutagus—was more than just a fantasy. My soul knew this man, loved him, but I didn't want to fall prey to passion. I didn't want to give in to the energy of Beltane. I wanted to be sure. Did our souls know one another as Boite's and Emer's had?

Banquo leaned in, took my face in both of his hands, and kissed me. First he kissed me gently, putting soft, sweet kisses on my lips. Then he grabbed me and pulled me hard against him. His tongue roved inside my mouth. I soaked up the softness of his lips, feeling the brush of the sharp stubble of hair on his face. He smelled so sweet, but even more, he felt so familiar. My heart was racing, my knees weak.

Banquo whispered in my ear. "I never felt this before. Nothing, nothing like this. I have seen lovely girls, danced, kissed, and felt magic before. But not until I stepped foot in this place have I felt anything like this. I know you," he whispered in my ear. "This place whispered your name. Am I right? All that red hair," he said, running his hand down my smooth, blue-black tresses, wound for the day with colorful ribbons, "Boudicca. My wife. My wife of old. I found you again."

I pulled back and looked at him, sucking my bottom lip in, entwining my fingers in his. "It's true. I felt it as well. That's why I brought you here. I wanted to see if you remembered too."

"But what is this place?" he asked again as he stepped toward the mound.

"The tomb of Boudicca."

Banquo froze and stood staring at the mound. I didn't know what he was seeing, what he was experiencing, but I could see from the expression on his face that it had moved him deeply. After a few moments, he turned and smiled at me.

"Let's go and dance and make merry. We are lucky. Let's revel in our luck. We found each other once again. I have you now, and I won't let you go," I told him.

"Promise it," he said, pulling me close, "Cerridwen, with the violet eyes, promise it with your soul."

I kissed him deeply then whispered in his ear. "I promise."

Banquo bent and plucked a small purple violet from the forest floor. Smiling, he stuck it behind my ear. I took his hand and lead him back to the coven. My visions were not fancy. I'd found my love once again.

NIGHT CAME QUICKLY. AND, AS before, the expected pairs disappeared. That evening, however, my mind was clear. I had drunk very little. Banquo and I stayed up talking very late.

"You'll leave in the morning," I said regretfully.

"Yes, but I will be back again at Samhain."

"You speak as if six months is a short time."

"Isn't it?"

"Not to me."

"It will pass quickly."

I smiled serenely and gazed into the fire, staring at the glowing red coals. The flames flickered and popped. My eyes felt drowsy and soon I thought I saw images in the light. It seemed that I could see myself in a grand castle hall, and I was shouting at the black-haired man I had seen in the cauldron. And, somehow, it seemed to me that Banquo was the reason for our quarrel.

"Cerridwen," Banquo said and shook my arm.

I pulled myself away from the image and looked at him.

"What did you see?"

I didn't want to tell him. With Banquo at my side, I had completely forgotten the dark-haired man. After all, what good to me was a phantom in comparison to the real, sweet flesh sitting beside me? Who was this ghost in my cauldron compared to Banquo, a noble Lord himself, for whom I felt an ancient pull. I felt with all my heart that I belonged to Banquo. I always had.

"The court life," I said in a half-truth.

"Will you rejoin the court one day?" Banquo asked. I heard the edge of excitement in his voice.

"I must."

"When we leave here, I ride north for a brief time to my father. I am...I am also of a noble house. I will inquire with my father on his plans," Banquo said cautiously.

"I..." I began, but I didn't know what to say. I dare not tell him who I was without talking to Madelaine first. I would have given him anything, my very soul, but I didn't dare do anything that would bring harm to Madelaine. I had to think of her too. "I need to talk to my family," I said.

Banquo smiled. "Then let us talk again. At Samhain."

We both sighed then giggled because we had done so. The rest of the evening we talked until our eyes could barely stay open any longer, and then we fell asleep in one another's arms.

The sun woke us, and the sound of the others packing the horses fell on unhappy ears.

Lamenting, I followed Banquo when he gave his goodbye to Epona. Afterward, he pulled me into his arms held me tight against his chest. His kisses grazed the top of my head. He lifted my unbandaged palm and looked into it. I followed his gaze.

"The Roma can look at the lines on one's hand and see the future. I cannot do so, but in my heart I am certain that I see myself here," he said and traced his finger down a line on my hand.

"Don't be so certain," I said, and took his hand and placed it over my heart, "because I was sure I saw you here."

He kissed my lips; it was a sweet, soft kiss of love.
"Well, son, will I have to pry you from Cerridwen's side?" Balor asked.

Banquo smiled. "Not for long, I hope."

"We shall see you in October?" Epona asked.

"Certainly," Balor answered.

"Then farewell and blessed be," Epona told them. Banquo mounted. I reached my hand out to him. He took it, squeezed it tight, and leaned toward me. "Tell your family I am Banquo of Lochaber. I will be Thane after my father, and I would have you as my bride. And the next time I come, I will ask my future wife's name," he said, smiling mischievously at me, then turned and rode away.

Fourteen

I SIGHED HEAVILY. I WASN'T SURE if Epona had heard
Banquo's words or not, but she said nothing. The
bards were leaving and goodbyes were being given. Not
having the heart for another farewell, I went to Sid's
house.

I knocked on her door. The door opened swiftly. She
pulled me inside before I could think of resisting and
banged the door shut behind me. We both watched in
horror as several objects—a brush, a cup, a scarf, and a
scroll—whirled around the room.

"What...what is this?" I stammered.

"Brownies. I can't get rid of them."

"Let me go get some snowdrops. I think Druanne
has some in—," I said and reached for the door handle,
but a brush came hurling at me. I ducked before it could
hit me in the face.

"Buggers," Sid shouted.

"Where is Nadia?"

"She went back through the barrow."

"Well, what now? How do you get rid of brownies?" I squinted around the room. I didn't see sign of the actual creatures themselves, just the items they had enchanted.

"Drive them away."

"How?"

"You must see them first. Call your wings. Do what you were taught, Raven Beak."

I closed my eyes, took a deep breath, and tried to calm my heart, which was slamming in my chest. At first all I could hear was Sid's upset breathing. "Scotia," I whispered in my mind. "I need you. Scotia?"

There was a distant, hollow, rustling sound. Faintly, I heard: "Yes?"

"Aid my eyes."

"It is within you, ancient one," she said in an echoing reply then the voice disappeared.

I slowly opened my eyes. The room shimmered gold. Then, I saw them. Neither fairy nor troll, brownies were kin of the fey folk somewhere in the middle. They were no more than six inches high, had wings like wasps, lionesque manes, and bushy tails like squirrels. Their skin was furred and spotted like spring fawns. They had small, wrinkled faces with long noses. When they saw me looking at them, really looking at them, they stopped and stared, their small black eyes gleaming.

I took a deep breath and felt my body, my power. My arms had become the wings of a raven, yet my body remained intact. I rose on my wings; the brownies scattered. They flew toward the fireplace and went up and out. As if I were translucent, I floated through the roof. The brownies balked to find me on the other side.

I laughed, and in a heartbeat, I overtook them. I flapped my raven wings on them, teasing them a bit. I didn't want to hurt them. I just wanted them to go. They zipped off on their tiny wings, never looking back. It was a warning. It was enough.

I opened my eyes. With a whooshing sensation, I floated back into my body. The wings were gone.

"My thanks," Sid said then went to pick up the fallen items. She looked up at me from under her long lashes. "Raven Beak," she said then chuckled, shaking her head.

"How is it you see all these things, them, me?" I whispered.

"I see what no one else wants to see."

"Yet you don't dislike or mistrust me. Druanne dislikes me."

Sid set the brush on her bureau. It was then that I realized her room was very beautiful. I hadn't noticed before, but Sid's room was decorated with fine furniture. The ornately carved bed, looking glass, and armoire inlaid with shells were all beautifully designed. As well, her bed was covered with heavy green velvet blankets and black bear furs. Her room was outfitted finer than my old chamber in Madelaine's castle. I was puzzled.

"First, for all her pomposity, Druanne lives in this world. She knows only the rules, the procedures. She never takes the next step into the unknown, to really feel the magic at the heart of it all. She says the words then calls it done. That is not the way of the Otherworld, so she does not understand the powers you possess. You are a protector of the land, as you have always been.

Because of the White Christ, the fey now live on the other side. I speak for them as best as I can, and it is time for some wrongdoing to come to an end. And second, dislike you? If I disliked you, why would I be back with you yet again?" Sid asked then laughed. "Besides, it has been a long time since anyone has understood me. I'm so thankful you're finally here. Ah, and here is Nadia," she said then looked toward her fireplace.

I followed her gaze. Floating before the fireplace, inside a capsule of golden light, was a tiny woman in a gown made of flower petals. She had long, bronze-colored hair strung with ribbons. She floated on tiny gossamer wings. The look of surprise on her face was a mirror of my own. Instantaneously, however, she disappeared. Nadia. I had seen her.

Fifteen

AFTER BELTANE, MY TRAINING IN the magical arts continued. Epona finished her lessons on Ogham then turned to the symbols carved into the standing stones by the ancient people of the land, the Picts. My father's blood was the blood of old Alba. I was descended from the woad-painted Picts. The first people here, the native people of this land, the Picts, practiced ancient and arcane magic. Engraved on stones, worked into embroidery, and even tattooed on bards, Pictish symbols were everywhere. I wanted to know what the symbols meant.

"Why do a husband and wife exchange a comb and mirror at their wedding?" Epona asked as we stood alone, deep in the forest, beside a large boulder. Epona had cleared away some lichen and fern to reveal that the stone was carved. On it were many symbols, boars, crescents, and a set of double discs, but it also had a comb and mirror carved thereon.

"I always thought it had something to do with the woman's beauty," I replied.

Epona smiled at me. "As do most people, but I want you to look at the actual objects," she said, and from her small bag she pulled out a small round hand mirror and a comb. She handed the comb to me.

"What is it made from?" she asked me.

I felt the pale-colored comb. On it, someone had engraved the image of a merwoman. "Bone."

"But what kind of bone?"

I shook my head. "Stag?"

"That is whale bone, a great creature of the sea. And, of course, you see the traditional merwoman carved thereon. Have you ever noticed there is always a merwoman or some sea creature carved on the comb?"

I nodded. She was right.

"The comb," she said, "is a symbol of the sea. If the ritual is performed properly, the comb is always made of whale bone and always decorated with water images." She took the comb from me and set it on the boulder. She then lifted the mirror to reflect my face. I had grown tan from my work in the smithy. The sunlight overhead made my black hair shimmer blue and brought out the violet color of my eyes. Behind me, the forest glowed vibrant green. "A woman, and her womb, is all earth, but around her is all spirit, air. She is ready. She is all. She is the fertile land. Around her is the air of heaven. But her womb cannot grow without—"

"Without seed...water," I said.

Epona lowered the mirror. "Land and sea. The mirror and the comb are fertility magic. They have nothing to do with beauty. They are a reflection of the two forces, male and female, that come together to bring life into the world, the land and sea merging to become one living force," Epona said then turned and touched the stone. "Someone married here." She reached out to touch the symbols. "In days long past, true love was pledged here. Long forgotten." She gently put the items back into her bag, and we headed back to the coven.

As we walked back, I could not help but think of Banquo. Would I be permitted to marry the Thane of Lochaber? Certainly, it was the title of a lesser house, but it was still a title. Maybe if Malcolm knew I had found someone I cared for, he would permit it. And certainly Banquo's father would never deny my family. I would have to entreat Madelaine. She would come soon. If Alister was really…dead…she would come soon.

BUT MADELAINE DIDN'T COME THAT day nor the next. What if my vision had been false? What if Alister was alive and well and still beating Madelaine every night? I couldn't stand the thought of it: her dislocated shoulders, broken lips, swollen eyes. It made me sick. It made me angry. So I waited, every day, praying she would come. Days turned into weeks and then months.

One day near midsummer, when I still pined for my aunt, Epona and I took the horses out for a ride so Epona could teach me rule of nines Madelaine had mentioned.

"The natural order of things comes in specific sets of numbers. Three is a holy number, as well you know. Even the priests of the White Christ know this with their

Father, Son, and Holy Spirit. It is interesting, no, that the Christians maintain a pantheon of gods, or a single god with three faces, but still call us heretical for having more than one god?"

"I am afraid I know very little of Christianity. Madelaine didn't permit the priests to teach me."

"Then you must read the holy writ of the White Christ."

I frowned.

"If you seek to help the Goddess, you must understand what mistruths and wrongdoings you are avenging. To do so, however, you must know their holy tales. You must learn Latin. It should be easy for you. You have a quick mind for languages."

I was often complimented on my beauty or my lineage, but rarely complimented for my mind. Epona's words made me smile; I felt proud.

We rode across the windswept Lowlands. The rolling fields spread across the land, a vista of shades of green: emerald, chartreuse, and sage. We'd left the woods and had been riding toward the east coast.

"Yet, I digress. Three is a holy number. It relates to the three faces of the Goddess. Nine, as well, is a holy number. A multiple of three, it is the number of the Queens of the Fisher King, and goes even further back to the old covens, such as the ones on Avalon, Hy Brasil, the Fortress of Shadows, and Atlantis. The number three also relates to the stone circles that dot our land. Your friend Banquo is riding from circle to circle to learn the mysteries of the stones. He walks where the worlds are thin, much like you do. That is why he wears the mark of the stag god. He has walked in the old worlds, encountered his god, and survived. Your Banquo is a rare talent," Epona said.

I could tell from the look on her face that she was bating me. But I didn't mind. Epona felt like a mother. I felt natural warmth and protectiveness coming from her.

"He is special," I replied.

"I am not certain that a match with Lochaber will be permitted. You must steel your heart, just in case. It is so painful to love someone but be given to another," she said, and for a moment, her brown-gold eyes looked far away.

Her words struck me. She was right. What if I we were denied? It would be hell to be married off to someone else. I couldn't stand the thought of it. I gazed at Epona. A single tear streamed down her cheek. She wiped it away. "Epona?"

"Once, long ago, such was my fate. A wild girl in love with a wild boy...given to a harsh old man in marriage," she said.

"I'm sorry for you," I told her, reaching out to touch her hand. "But you're here now. What of your wild boy? I mean, if you are here now, perhaps he—"

"He is long dead." Epona cleared her throat then painted on a smile again. "Yes, all that is long past. But remember, dear Cerridwen, no one is married on Beltane," she said with a smile. "Now, besides three, four is also a number of significance: four seasons, four elements. Fire, of course, is the most volatile of all the elements. It creates energy in a quick and forceful way. Even the priests of the White Christ can sense the power of fire. That is why candles burn on their alters. The power in fire can bring images to the mind and help one divine the future. Have you ever seen images in fire?"

I nodded.

"What did you see?"

"Recently, myself and a man. We were arguing."

"Have you seen this man before?"

"Not in the flesh, but I have seen him...in the cauldron. It was the Wyrd Sisters who first showed him to me." Their words haunted me. Your King, they had called him. But did they mean that he would be King of Scotland, ruler over us all, or would he be *my* King?

"Go cautiously with the Wyrd Sisters. They have their eyes on you but they plot and meddle, at times where they should not. Heed my word and be careful."

I nodded. Epona was right. I sensed their old, dark magic. It had a hint of danger to it. "And once, in the fire, I saw a vision of ravens in the snow, bloody snow, when my father died."

"Then the talent for divination lies in you. Not surprising. Use this power. Practice it. If the power to see the future lies in your hands, it is a great tool. Never trust the Wyrds blindly. Always seek answers for yourself. Fire, of course, is not the only diviner. Water can also show the future. Water and air are essential elements. The winds, however, come from four directions, and those directions each have a specific function. When the wind comes from the north it can mean death or change. An east wind indicates wisdom. A south wind is a powerful wind. A west wind is fertile and love-giving. And, finally, we come to earth. Earth is the embodiment of fertility. Think of it; we put a seed in the ground, it grows, from it springs food that allows us to live. To me, that is magic."

Epona directed her mare up the hill. When we reached the top we found ourselves at the shoreline. Far below us was a sandy shore and dark blue water. It was beautiful. I looked behind me to see the horizon rolling with fat hills.

"Look. There is a ship," Epona said and pointed out toward the water.

We dismounted.

Epona plucked some grass. The wind took it and pulled it behind us. "We have a west wind." She then took my left hand and lifted it above our heads. She raised her other hand. I mimicked her.

"We call you, wind of the west, wind of love and fertility, and we offer you our love and respect in exchange for your power."

We both stilled, and the wind continued to blow around us.

"We ask for a fair wind if those upon that ship are friends to our land and country. If those upon that ship mean to do ill to our kinsmen, then whip up your strength and banish them from the sea!"

I channeled my power into Epona's words, closing my eyes, and let my body feel the wind around me. At first it blew erratically, but then began to blow strong and steady. A firm, good wind pushed from the land to the sea, lending its power to the ship's sails. In my mind's eye, I could see the wind whipping around me, sparkling gold.

Epona brought our hands down.

I opened my eyes. "Friend," I said as I looked out at the water.

Epona nodded and pulled a wine flask from her saddle bag. She took a long drink and handed the skin to me. We rested quietly, and after awhile decided it was time to turn back.

My mind was lost to my thoughts as we rode back. Epona, too, was quiet. I couldn't help but wonder if she was thinking about her wild boy. Who had Epona been before this place?

I sighed heavily. So much was happening. I knew I had come to the grove for training, but I had not expected…well, all of this. It was far beyond any girlish expectation. I felt awed by the world that had opened itself to me. I felt strength under my skin I'd never felt before. That strength made me feel powerful. I felt alive. I felt anger and lust. It was almost like pieces of myself were collecting themselves back to me once again. When I was with Sid, I felt more solid. Banquo ignited feelings I had only ever dreamed of. He was *my* wild boy, a druid who walked between the worlds. I wanted to be with him…and with Sid. I wanted there to be a place, a world, where we could all be together. I wanted to feel Cerridwen, and the raven wings, and be that part of myself living just under my skin. What would that place look like? What would that life look like? If my visions were true, that life would look like the life of Queen Boudicca, and it was a life I'd already lived.

sixteen

I WAS NOT VISITED AGAIN BY the Wyrd Sisters all that summer, but I remembered my visits to them and began practicing their art. I sought visions in the flames or in the cauldron, looking for what I knew and what I didn't. Mostly I sought Sid, when she was away from the coven, Madelaine, and Banquo. Once I found Madelaine at Malcolm's court, the King looking at his half-sister with disinterest. Sid was harder to find. She always appeared like a shimmering silhouette surrounded by hues of green. There were people, glimmering people, near her, laughing, but I could never quite make anyone out. When I found Banquo, I could not see where he was, but around him I often saw darkness and fire. Sometimes I would catch glimpses of the black-haired man, usually at the side of his blond-haired warrior giant friend and at sea. Despite the Wyrd Sister's words about him being my King, my curiosity had faded. I wanted Banquo, not a phantom.

Thora was growing into her fat little feet, and with the passage of time, she had grown several inches. As Banquo had mentioned, I began teaching her how to track. I started with little things, just hiding objects in my cabin and letting her find them. It wasn't very long until she seemed expert at the task.

Thora and I were not the only ones growing, changing. It was harvest season. Just days before the autumnal equinox, I woke to find Gwendelofar crying. She was curled up on her bed.

"What's wrong?" I asked.

"Oh, Cerridwen," she whispered. "I'm sorry. I didn't mean to wakes you."

I slid out of my bed and on hers. I put my arm around her. "What's happened? Should I get Epona?"

Gwendelofar shook her head.

"What is it, sister?"

"I'm pregnant," she whispered. "I want the child, but I'll have to leave, and I have nowhere to go."

"The father? It's...Sigurd?"

She nodded glumly. "Oh Cerridwen, think I loves him, but I don't know where he is or if he loves me! My child is a Beltane babe!"

Gwendelofar was shaking. I took her hands. "Sigurd will be here for the harvest festival any day now. Talk to him. Tell him your feelings. Perhaps he feels the same. The child *is* merry-begot, which means it will be a special child. Perhaps Sigurd will want to raise the child with you."

"I don't know," Gwendelofar said sadly.

On Beltane, any child conceived is a child of the Stag God, the Father God, the wild man of the forest, not the human father. The human father could not claim and had no right to a merry-begot babe. This also meant the father had no responsibility toward that child. It would solely be on choice, both Sigurd's and Gwendelofar's, if they should raise the child together.

"Well, soon you will learn. If not, you will raise the child yourself. Madelaine can find a place for you and your child in her household."

"Really? You're sure?"

"Yes," I said without hesitation. Knowing Madelaine, I knew I didn't even have to ask. And with Alister gone, it would be a safer place. Or at least I hoped.

"Fate gives me a mixed blessing," she whispered, wiping away a tear.

"That's something fate likes to do," I answered. I thought of my own mixed blessings—how much I loved Madelaine, but how much I wished I could have been raised by my own parents. But then I remembered, when it had been put to the question, I had once chosen Madelaine over Boite.

That cold winter eve when I had found my father in the snow, we rode back to Alister's castle, surprising an unsuspecting Madelaine. My father convinced Tavis and I not to announce his arrival. He wanted to surprise his sister.

"This way, father," I told him, trying to hide the excitement in my voice as I led my father down the hallway to the small sitting room where Madelaine and the others sat sewing beside the fire.

I kept turning again and again to look at him. He was so enormous, like a giant bear in his furs. He smiled kindly at me. Every time I looked at him, I searched his face for myself. And every time, be it the shape of his nose, the line of his brow, or his eyes, I found traces of myself there. When I was with my father, it made me feel like I actually belonged somewhere, to someone. I loved Madelaine, but she was not truly my mother.

"Wait here," I told my father as I pushed open the chamber door.

Madelaine looked up at me. "Corbie, I've been worried. Where did you fly off to, Little Raven?"

"I went to get a present for you."

"For me?" She set down her sewing and looked at me. "What do you have today? Let me see!"

"It's quite large," I told her. "Close your eyes."

The other ladies in the room suddenly became interested.

Madelaine giggled. "All right, my dear," she said then closed her eyes.

I opened the door to let my father in. I put my finger to my lips, shushing the other women in the room who all gasped when I led Boite inside. I led him to stand in front of Madelaine.

"Ready?" I asked.

Madelaine wrinkled her nose. "I smell snow."

"Open your eyes," I told her.

When Madelaine opened her eyes, a shocked expression crossed her face. She dropped everything and jumped up, wrapping her arms around her brother's neck. Boite had to hold her by the waist to keep her up.

"My brother!" she said excitedly. "My brother! Why have you come? Is anything the matter?"

Taking their cue, the waiting women picked up their belongings and left.

"Here, come close to the fire," she told him, pulling a chair near the hearth. She pushed him into the seat then began unlacing his boots. "You're chilled to the bone. Warm your feet by the flames. Corbie, get you daddy a mulled wine," she told me, sending me scrambling. "Is it Malcolm? Has he died? Alister? He was at court. Has anything happened to him? Is war coming?"

"Sister, sister," Boite said with a laugh. "Peace, sister. I do come with family news, but the news is fair," he said.

I poured a mulled wine from the copper decanter sitting by the fire and handed it to my father. He took the drink from me then kissed my hand.

I stood behind Madelaine and watched.

"I've a new wife," he said then.

Madelaine stopped for a moment, her hands growing still. She didn't look up.

Boite drank his wine. "Northern girl. A daughter of Moray. She's quite young. I've got her at Malcolm's court. I've come...I've come to see if Gruoch would like to join her stepmother."

For a moment, Madelaine said nothing. "*If* she would like?"

I stared at both of them. What did he mean he had a new wife? Would he really take me to Malcolm's court? Would I really join the royal household? Certainly, I deserved to be there as much as anyone. But how could I leave Madelaine?

"I've no wish to break the hearts of the two women I love most in this world. It is Gruoch's choice. I would not abuse either of you by forcing my will on the matter."

Boite looked from Madelaine to me. His eyes were soft. The awkwardness of the situation struck all of us. My father wanted me. I could live the life of a royal girl, be exposed to all the niceties of court rather than the debauchery of this castle. I could be near him. And in exchange, I would leave the woman who raised and loved me.

Madelaine turned at looked at me. "Don't answer now. Think it over," she said then looked back at her brother. "Tell us about your new wife," she said then, pulling off Boite's boots.

"Aedha. She's a wee lass. Pleasant spirit, but not hardy stock. I had expected more from Moray. She is sweet and kind."

Madelaine nodded. "Is she one of us?" she asked. One of us. Madelaine used the phrase from time to time. One of us, a follower of the old ways, those who carry on the belief in the ancient things.

Boite shook his head. "There are not so many of us left, dear sister."

I stared at them. My father wanted me. He wanted me with him. My heart sung. But then I looked at Madelaine. I had grown up under her watchful eyes, felt her loving kisses. Madelaine had always put me first. How many times had she taken a blow from Alister then straightened her back and attended to my needs with no thought for herself. There was nothing worse I could have done to Madelaine then leave her.

"I'll stay with Madelaine," I blurted out, interrupting their conversation.

They both turned and looked at me.

"Are you certain?" Madelaine asked. "The court life would be a good life for you. You would be able to get to know everyone, grow up amongst the royal ladies, alongside your cousins."

I shook my head. "I'll stay here," I told Madelaine whose eyes watered. I turned to my father. "If you'll pardon me, father, I will stay with Madelaine."

My father smiled at me. "Praise the gods you love each other so well. As you will, Little Raven. But should you ever wish to come, you are welcome."

Fate. Fate had offered me my father. But my will had trumped all. I stayed with Madelaine until the Goddess called. And my father and his new bride...both were dead before I ever had the chance to make good on his invitation. If I had known that visit would be his last, I might have chosen a different fate.

seventeen

TWO DAYS AFTER I FOUND Gwendelofar in tears, the bards arrived to celebrate the autumnal equinox. It had been a magnificent growing season. We had a bounty of food. Every day leading up to the celebration, Druanne had us all harvesting herbs, gourds, grains, and all manner of foods. Uald brought home fish and wild game. All of our houses and the coven square were filled with flower cuttings. Gwendelofar worked with Druanne to extract plant and flower oils. She came home smelling like flowers.

I was in the square preparing a broth with Uald when the bards arrived. Epona came out to give greetings.

"My friends! Welcome back," she called.

Uald, her hands sticky with fish guts, smiled in welcome.

I saw Sigurd scan the coven grove. Aridmis and Druanne were crossing the lawn to join us, but Gwendelofar was still inside our little cabin. She had been napping all morning. Something told me fate was going to need a little help. I set down the onion I'd been cutting, wiped my hands on the skirt of my once-lovely green gown, now worn to tatters, and went to Sigurd. I took the reins of his horse while he dismounted.

"Ah, sister Cerridwen. Pleasure to see you again! Where is Gwen?" he asked, and I saw a glimmer of worry cross his face. Was he worried she was gone? Maybe he did care for her after all.

"Within," I said, motioning back to my house. "Let's go surprise her," I said with a smile.

I handed Sigurd's horse's reins to Brant. "Lady Cerridwen," he greeted with a smile.

"Welcome back," I said nicely then led Sigurd across the lawn to the little home I shared with Gwendelofar. I could feel the eyes of my sisters, who now all knew Gwendelofar's condition, on us. I felt a bit bad for Sigurd. I knew Gwendelofar would find a happy life for her and her child with or without him, but I could feel the hopes of the women around me…and Druanne's judgment.

I opened the door to my house. Gwendelofar was sleeping. The sunlight was just shining through the window and cast a scattering of light on her golden hair. Her cheeks were rosy. She wore a pale pink gown, a simple thing that she had embroidered around the neckline with small blue flowers.

I heard Sigurd gasp at the sight of her. Her belly had just begun to show.

"I'll go," I whispered. "You wake her."

"Are you certain?" he said nervously then looked at me. He was such a hulking figure. His muscular and tattooed arms peeking out from under his tunic, his wild hair woven into braids, and he had grown a beard since we'd last seen him, as most men did as winter approached. He was the very picture of a warrior. But his voice trembled. I realized then that no matter what, the Goddess wields her own power. Love, beauty, sex, these powers belong to the Goddess in us all. Lying there the picture of beautiful, blossoming in motherhood, Gwendelofar's power emanated from her even as she slept. Sigurd and Gwendelofar were a great match.

I took his hand. "I am. It will please her so. May the Gods bless you both," I said, then grabbing a bag filled with my clothing that I had packed in anticipation of his arrival, I quietly left.

I would stay at Sid's house, I'd decided. I took my pack and crossed the lawn. Quietly and carefully entering Sid's home, hoping to find no Brownies within, I went inside. I was surprised to find Sid lying on her bed.

She was a sorry sight. She was extremely dirty. Her feet were bloodied. Her hair was all tangles. He dress was torn. I had not seen her in several weeks. I dropped my pack and went to her. I lifted her wrist to feel for her heartbeat. It was faint.

"Sid?" I whispered.

She did not stir.

I shook her shoulder. "Sid?"

She groaned a little.

"Sidhe, wake," I whispered, kneeling down by her bed.

She opened her eyes a little. "Cerridwen?"

"What happened?"

"I haven't eaten," she whispered.

I rose and poured her a glass of water. Pulling her up in bed, I helped her drink. After she'd drunk the full glass, I went outside and retrieved a bowl of broth. Lifting spoonful after spoonful, I fed her.

"It's so hard to remember the passage of time," she whispered.

"Why are your feet in such a state?" I asked.

"I got lost," she answered quietly.

"Lost?"

"I traveled far. I wasn't certain where I was."

"How long have you been back?" I asked.

"A couple of days."

"A couple of days!"

"I couldn't…" she said and then paused. "I couldn't rise."

I went to her small fireplace and stoked a fire. I set a small pot of water to warm beside it. Once it was heated, I wet a rag and began washing Sid's cut and bruised feet. She cringed but let me clean them. When I was finished, I went to Epona's house and retrieved salve and clean bandages. Sid had fallen asleep sitting up. I applied the salve, the sharp scent of the herbs making my nose tingle, and then wrapped her feet. She never woke.

A few minutes later, Druanne rapped lightly on the door. "I thought I saw you come in here with bandages," she said as she slowly opened the door. I watched her eyes quickly assess the situation. "Damn her. She is never careful enough."

"I've bandaged her feet, gotten some food into her, and her heart has quickened."

In a huff, Druanne turned around. "I'll be right back," she said, slamming the door behind her.

Sid slept on.

Druanne returned with a flask. "It's a sweet mixture which will quicken her blood and wake her." She moved to rouse Sid.

"She has food in her belly. Let her sleep a bit longer," I said.

Druanne frowned at me.

"I'll wake her in a while."

"You should have let me know. I am your elder. I am trained in the healing arts. I know better than you what to do," Druanne said then shook Sid's shoulder, waking her.

"Don't underestimate me. Epona has taught me as well."

"Willful girl, your power is reckless."

"What do you know of my power?" I glared at her.

Sid woke somewhat. Druanne held her jaw, a bit too roughly for my liking, and poured the liquid down her throat. Sid sputtered a little.

Druanne patted her back, helping the liquid clear, then lay her back down. "I know your power is more harmful than good, that's what I know."

"You fear it because it showed me your true nature. You have no reason to be afraid of me. I wouldn't strike at you unless you gave me a reason."

"Fear you? I hardly fear you. You simply don't belong here," Druanne said, and in a huff, she rose and left, slamming the door behind her once again.

"Try not to peck her eyes out, Raven Beak," Sid said in a whisper.

"I'm doing my best," I assured her, glaring at the door.

Sid laughed softly.

"You smell horrible. Let me get this dirty thing off you," I told Sid.

She nodded, and with my help, she sat up. I pulled her old gown, a tattered black cotton dress, off her. It smelled so bad and was in such a shamble that I set it aside to be burnt. I went back to the fire, warmed some wash water, then grabbed the sweet smelling lemon balm soap Sid had sitting on her bureau.

Sid lay naked in her bed. She was drowsy, her eyes opening and closing softly. I covered her body and washed the grime from her legs. She was a thin woman, but her legs were muscular. I washed her arms. They were a mess of scratches and grime.

"Where did you get all this fine furniture, anyway?" I asked her as I cleaned her up.

"A gift...from the Seelie King when our son was born," Sid whispered absently.

"Your son, is he—"

"Eochaid."

"Eochaid?"

"My son," Sid said quietly. "His name is Eochaid. He's so beautiful."

"Like his mother," I said as I gently washed the dirt smudges from her face.

Sid smiled. Her eyes closed.

I gently pulled the cover away and washed her soft, white stomach. My eyes were drawn again and again to her small, pert breasts with their soft pink nipples. My mind went back to the day at the spring with Banquo.

Sid rolled over and looked at me. She took the rag from my hands and pulled me onto the bed beside her. Despite her exhaustion, she leaned forward to press her mouth against mine. I could taste the potion Druanne had given her, the sweet taste of honey, marigold, chamomile, and other herbs lingering in her mouth. I kissed her gently, again and again, tasting her. My hands shaking, I gently touched her breasts, my fingers grazing those small, sweet nipples which hardened to my touch. It was not the power of Beltane guiding me. It was something different, an old longing. I wanted to feel her body close to mine, but I knew she was weak. I removed my clothes pulled her against me, enveloping her in my embrace. It felt so good to feel our skin touching. Sid kissed my neck and gently stroked my body. Her touch felt wonderful, so sweet, so familiar. Sighing deeply, she laid her head on my chest and entwined her fingers around mine.

"Now we just need Banquo," she whispered, and moments later, she fell asleep.

A COUPLE OF DAYS LATER, we all reveled in the celebration of two things: the harvest and the handfasting of Gwendelofar and Sigurd. Sid was still not well enough to join us. Most of the time she slept. I stayed by her side as much as I could, but joined the others for the wedding celebration.

Gwendelofar was dressed splendidly. Aridmis had surprised us all a day earlier when she emerged from her house with a wedding gown to give to Gwendelofar.

"I was my mother's," she'd told us. "I will never have the chance to wear it. My life is here. Wear it in good health," she told Gwendelofar.

"Oh, no! I cannot. One day maybe you—"

Aridmis shook her head. "No, I will not. My life is here," Aridmis repeated again with finality. From her words, we all understood that Aridmis knew her fate and was resigned to it.

"Thank you," Gwendelofar said, tears welling in her eyes.

I stood with the others at the center of the coven, the fire burning brightly. We said our prayers and listened attentively while Epona performed the marriage rite. Near the end of the ceremony, Epona pulled out the same comb and mirror she had shown me, handing the comb to Gwendelofar and the mirror to Sigurd.

"By the Lord and the Lady, exchange these tokens of marriage and become...not two in one union...but three. The earth is fertile," Epona said.

Sigurd handed the mirror to Gwendelofar.

"And the seed is sewn," Epona added.

Gwendelofar handed the comb to Sigurd.

Epona then pulled out a long cord of red ribbon. The couple held the marriage talismans as Epona wove the ribbon around their hands, beginning the wrap on Gwendelofar's arm, circling until the ribbon was tightly wound on Sigurd's arm.

"I unite you. God and Goddess. Husband and Wife. Mother and Father," Epona said, touching Gwendelofar's stomach gently. "You are now one. In life and in spirit. May the great ones bless you."

"So mote it be!" we all called happily.

"So mote it be," Gwendelofar and Sigurd answered in unison, and then they kissed, sealing their wedlock.

By the next morning, Gwendelofar and her husband had gone. Sigurd would take his wife and unborn child north to his small farm. In my heart, I wished her well. Fate, in the end, had been kind.

eighteen

IN LATE SEPTEMBER, WE HEARD the sound of hooves coming toward the coven. Madelaine's red hair shone through the trees, most of their leaves now fallen. Uald and I had been practicing at swordplay in the coven square while Sid watched on. Dressed in riding breeches and a night shirt cut off at the waist, I was a little embarrassed to have Madelaine see me. Not to mention, I was completely soaked in sweat.

"Seems I've left my niece here too long already," Madelaine said with a smile from atop her horse. "She's a doppelganger of you!" she told Uald with a laugh.

"Even worse," Uald said. "She's already better than me."

I slid the sword into its scabbard and crossed the lawn to join my aunt. I smiled at Uald's compliment. It was an elaboration, but my daily sparring had improved a lot. I was getting good. I held Madelaine's horse's bridle while she dismounted. She practically leapt from her horse, catching me into a fast hug, squeezing and kissing me.

"I've missed you so much," she told me.

"Me too," I replied, kissing her cheek.

Madelaine cupped my face in her hands and studied me. "How beautiful you are."

I smiled back at her then turned to Sid. "Madelaine, have you met Sid?" I asked, turning to Sid who had, apparently, been talking to Nadia. When I said her name, Sid ended her conversation with the invisible fairy woman, frowning at her with annoyance.

Sid smiled. "I've heard so much about you."

Madelaine took Sid's hand and smiled at her, but I saw Madelaine's brow furrow as though she was puzzled. "Have we met before?"

Sid smiled knowingly. "No, we haven't." Sid then frowned and shushed Nadia. "Not now," she whispered to her invisible companion.

Madelaine looked puzzled.

"Epona is out riding," I said. "She should be back soon."

Uald, also drenched in sweat, caught Madelaine up in her arms, lifting her off the ground.

Madelaine laughed loudly. "Put me down!"

Sid then fell into an argument with Nadia. The fight ended when Sid sighed loudly. "I'll be back soon," Sid told me then headed off into the woods.

"Come. We'll wait for Epona," Uald said, motioning to her little home at the back of the smithy. I tied Madelaine's horse to a post then followed Uald inside.

Uald slid her tools into a box, wiping the table clean with her hands, then motioned for us to sit while she poured us both an ale.

"There is much to say," Madelaine intimated with a serious look on her face. She took my hands. "Alister is dead, and I have been remarried."

Uald's slammed the mugs down angrily. Ale sloshed over the top. "They treat you like a common whore, pushing you on one man and then another."

Madelaine looked at her with soft eyes. "It is the way of things."

"To whom are you married?" I asked.

"To the Mormaer of Fife. He is an old man, kind and sweet, enamored with his new, young wife."

I smiled and squeezed Madelaine's hands. Alister was dead. My vision was true. He was dead. And I had killed him. I had released Madelaine from her pain and punished a man most deserving of punishment.

"So Fife and Lothian are now locked," Uald grunted as she threw herself into a chair. She propped her feet up on the table and drank deeply from her mug.

Madelaine nodded.

"Who made the marriage match?" Uald asked.

"King Malcolm," Madelaine said, "and he asked after you, Corbie."

It took me a moment to respond to that name.

"Ah, you would no longer be Corbie, would you? What do they call you now, my sweet?"

"Cerridwen."

Madelaine thought it over. "A dark goddess. It fits you. Your father would be proud," she said with a smile.

The thought that my father would be proud of me made me smile, but the notion that the King was making inquiries had made my heart beat faster, and worry gripped my stomach. "What did King Malcolm ask?" "He asked your age, your looks, your welfare, and your whereabouts."

"He's considering marrying her off too?" Uald hissed.

"He's planning."

"Did you see Duncan?"

Madelaine nodded. "He's fair-haired and gangly. I'm not sure there is much of a mind is rattling behind those eyes. His mother was always dim-witted. I don't see any of the MacAlpin blood in the boy."

Duncan was not the black-haired man I had seen in my cauldron, then. I had wondered, given it was known Duncan was slated to be king, if he was mystery phantom who'd haunted my visions. But if the raven-haired man wasn't Duncan, who was he?

"I'm glad your new husband is kind," I told Madelaine and shifted, unsure how to broach a new topic but wanting badly to interrupt the last. "Aunt, there has been an inquiry for my hand in marriage."

"An inquiry? How? From who?"

Uald smiled smugly but lifted her mug of ale so Madelaine wouldn't see.

"A druid…a young man who visited here. I was quite taken with him. He will be the Thane of Lochaber. He has asked that he be considered."

"You told him who you were?" Madelaine looked alarmed.

I shook my head. "Only that I am from a noble house, like him." I smiled as I thought about Banquo. If the marriage could be arranged, I could travel to Lochaber with Banquo after Samhain.

Madelaine smiled softly. "You are young, my dear. At your age, the flame of love can fan quickly. There are many Lords who are inquiring for your hand. And many Lords with titles far above Thane of Lochaber."

I frowned at Madelaine's words. I was young, and Banquo and I had just met, but that didn't mean what I felt wasn't real. "It is a noble and powerful house."

"Ruled over by Gillacoemgain, Mormaer of Moray, who is also unwed and has begun making inquiries. I don't know Malcolm's plans, but there is great strife in the north. Thorfinn the Mighty, as they call him, is gaining power over the northern-most provinces but is backed by Norway. Something will be done to quell him, by war or marriage.

She took a drink and continued, "And Thorfinn fosters Lord Macbeth, your cousin Donalda's son. With Macbeth's father dead, at the hands of the Mormaer of Moray mind you, he too holds sway in the north. The matter is desperately convoluted.

"But what I know for sure is that Duncan, Macbeth, Thorfinn, and Gillacoemgain are all unwed. All four have a claim on the north. All four would be a strong marriage match for the daughter of Boite. And all four would rule over the Thane of Lochaber."

"But…I love him." It was true. I did love Banquo. He was my soulmate.

"What is his name, this druid who has charmed you?"

"Banquo."

Madelaine looked at Uald who was smirking. "Well?"

"He is a good lad, and he is a druid. And he bears the marks of the stag god. He is well-suited for this dark goddess, and the two of them would be a stronghold for our faith. Ignore the duties of your line and follow the duties of your religion. Move Malcolm. Convince him on the match. Cerridwen is right. Lochaber is a strong province and a good ally. Perhaps the king would consider it since love is involved."

"Malcolm is not moved by sentiment."

"Let Malcolm take the north by force. Lochaber could stand with him and raise the isles, their ally, to Malcolm's banner."

Madelaine looked thoughtful. "He doesn't know who you are? You are certain?"

I nodded.

"That helps. Malcolm has enough of the old blood in him to hear me out. He knows where you truly are. He will understand how you and this Banquo came together. I will do what I can. Lochaber has always been friendly to our line. Their Thane would want the marriage for his son, but I cannot promise anything. My Little Corbie, you must realize you are the last gem in Malcolm's treasure chest, the last little bird he can marry off to win him an alliance. You must not get your hopes up, but I will do my best."

I sighed heavily.

Madelaine took my hands and smiled gently at me. And I realized, for the first time in my remembrance, no ghosts lived behind her eyes. I saw no bruises anywhere on her. It was finally over. I was happy for her, but I worried for myself. Surely, Banquo and I were meant to be together. Nothing could stand in the way of such old soul magic, could it?

Epona arrived a few hours later. Madelaine shared her news with her.

"I will be moving my household to Fife. Malcolm will put someone from Alister's line in place. I won't be far, but when you return, you will come to Fife."

"So the Thane of Fife has another wife," Epona said. "His history with his brides is not good."

"I am his fifth wife, but he is not Alister. I quizzed the household women hard on the matter. All the others died in childbirth, by accident, or in sickness. There were no questions, just misfortune. The Thane is a fat old man looking for a pretty woman to sit beside him and tell him jokes. He has done his duty in the bedroom once or twice but doesn't seek it. He is in his gray years. He seeks a companion."

"Speaking of? What of Tavis?" I asked.

"He is part of my household. He will accompany me to Fife."

I smiled. I was so glad.

It was late in the evening when Madelaine finally took our leave.

"I promise you I will inquire as soon as I can on this matter with Lochaber," she told me.

I kissed Madelaine on the cheek then buried my nose in her hair. I had missed her smell; she smelled like hyacinths and home.

"I love you," she whispered.

"I love you too," I replied.

Madelaine, accompanied by Uald, who would journey with her to the stream, rode out of the coven.

I sent a silent prayer out to the Goddess: *let the King be swayed. Let me marry the Thane of Lochaber.*

The only reply I got in return was silence.

nineteen

FALL DRIFTED AWAY. THE HILLS turned purple with heather and then back to a dingy brown. It was not long before the cold winter winds began to whip. The fresh fruits and vegetables disappeared from our table and were replaced by potted foods, meats, and breads.

At the end of October, we began preparing for the Samhain celebration, and I began counting the days until Banquo returned. There had been no word from Madelaine. I didn't know if she'd yet spoken to Malcolm. A holiday for dark magic, Samhain marked the eve when the veil between the worlds would be the thinnest. And it was the night most sacred to the dark goddesses. I waited on Samhain, but the days before dragged on with excruciating slowness.

"How did you stand living in the castle? If I spend even a few days walled up I begin to feel my mind slip," Sid complained as she paced her room one evening.

"I didn't think about it much, and I had Madelaine to entertain me."

"Mad Elaine, Mad Elaine, ever full of life. Let's pass the time. Want to learn how to send a casting? I know you've done it before, but you can never practice too much, Raven Beak."

I nodded.

"Then lie down," she said and crawled onto her bed. She grinned at me.

I smirked at Sid. We'd never said anything about what had passed between us. Sid acted as if nothing unusual had happened, but I'd begun to see her in a different light. I adored her, and she was intimately tied to Banquo, whom I loved. I wanted to marry Banquo, to be his bride, to bear his children. I wanted to rule Lochaber at his side. With Sid, I just wanted to be with her. We belonged together, her and me and Banquo. The three of us. When Sid lay down, I felt a strong urge to touch her, to put my lips and hands on her, to feel that wild energy inside her. To feel her. When I thought about it, I wondered about the deep affection I saw between Uald and Madelaine, and wondered if it was similar.

"Not now," Sid said with a grin. "Lie down and learn something."

"I'm fairly certain I learned a few things the last time I lay down on this bed," I said with a wink.

Sid laughed, reached over, and pinched me. "Pay attention, Raven Beak. What you must do is lift out of your body. Rise up without moving a muscle. You will have complete control of where you go. You will not be at the whim of chance. I've seen you do it before. Go ahead and try."

I looked at Sid. "But how?"

"Ride the silver thread as you did in the barrow when you visited the Wyrd Sisters or glide on your raven wings. Close your eyes and rise up as you did before. But rise up and out of your body."

I tried to quiet my mind, which still rumbled with thoughts of Sid's soft skin and fiery touch. After some time, I became still and focused on my breathing, on the beating of my heart. I pulled my energy in and focused. I focused on my soul. I tried to see Sid's room through my mind's eye. I thought about the moon. Determined to look at the glowing orb, I bade myself sit up. And I did. I saw the room around me and Sid lying beside me. I rose, walked to the window, and gazed out at the silvery disc. It was nearly full. In two weeks it would be Samhain.

"See," Sid said. "You've done it with no trouble at all."

I turned around. Our bodies lay on the bed. Sid stood beside herself. It was different, much different, from when I had traveled to the Wyrd Sisters. And this time, I did not have my raven wings. I was myself, but in spirit. And this time, I was in control.

"Is this how you usually go the faerie?" I asked.

"Sometimes. Sometimes I go to them whole as I did that day in the barrow."

"How did you do that?"

"I saw the portal to their world. Sometimes it is a glowing light. Sometimes there is a door. It is easier to walk between the world as sold flesh when you are in the old holy places, cairns, circle stones, or even caves. There are many caves in our realm that lead to dark, old places. They are guarded by the little people of the hollow hills who will trick you and kill you if they can. That's how I got lost at the autumn festival. They turned me around in the caves, and I emerged far from here. They are dark, old, and dangerous things."

"What are they?"

"Not human. Not faerie. Old. Ancient. From another world and time," she said. I couldn't help but notice her tremble. "Come, let's send before we grow too tired."

"Send?"

"Who do you want to see?" she asked.

"Banquo," I said right away.

She smiled.

It was strange to exist as a specter. I lifted my hands and saw through them. The world outside my window was silver.

"Where do you suppose Banquo is?" Sid asked.

"Somewhere north, or on his way here."

"Think then. See him. Find him. There is a tie between you and him. It is strong. Feel that pull and follow it."

I closed my eyes and thought about Banquo. I suddenly became warm, as if I was standing near a fire. I smelled men's bodies and ale. The heat was stifling. It made me feel heavy with sleep. I cracked my eyes open and saw a roaring fire in the center of a hall. Men slept on the floor under heavy furs. The wind outside whipped at the doors, but the heat backed the chill away. I opened my eyes more fully and looked around. I noticed Balor sleeping near the fire. My eyes sought out Banquo. He was half-awake, half-drunk sitting on a stool in front of the hearth. I walked toward him. He spied movement and looked up. At first he squinted, as if he could not see me clearly, then his eyes opened wide.

"Cerridwen?" he whispered.

Could I speak? "Hello, Love."

He paled. "Is something wrong?"

"All is well. It is only that I missed you. Are you coming soon?"

"Lord Thorfinn has just given us his leave. We ride south in the morning."

"This is the stronghold of Thorfinn the Mighty?"

Banquo nodded.

Another man stirred and sat up. He stared at me. He had long black hair, a long black beard peppered with white, and a sharp gaze. He wore black robes and had the pelt of a fox draped over his head. Around his neck, however, we wore a medallion carved with runes; it was the badge of a skald.

"Soon then," I whispered to Banquo and pulled back. As if I was being reeled in like I fish, I felt my energy snap back, and I stood once again in Sid's room. Her shadow was waiting. Both of our bodies still lay on the bed.

"You spoke to him?" she asked.

I nodded.

"Let's go back to ourselves before you tire too much," she said.

"How?"

"Don't look at your body, simply lie back into it."

Looking out the window, I lay back down on the bed, lying back into myself. I heard a loud noise as I took a sharp inhale. Suddenly, my flesh felt solid. I felt my heart. It was beating very softly. After a moment, Sid took a similar breath. She rolled over and rested her head on my chest.

"There was another man there who was able to see me," I whispered.

"Besides Banquo?" Sid asked, lacing her fingers in mine.

"A skald. Banquo is north with Lord Thorfinn. They will leave in the morning to join us."

"Thorfinn is said to have a gifted seer who travels with him. Those with the gift can see you when you cast."

"That must have been him then," I said and closed my eyes. "I feel so tired. And dizzy."

"It's always like that after a casting," Sid replied. Her voice sounded distant. "You'll get more used to it, but it always wears you out."

I wanted to reply but was too weak. I snuggled closer to Sid, inhaling the scent of lemon balm soap in her hair, and fell asleep, the moonlight casting silver rays down on us.

twenty

IN THE DAYS BEFORE THE Samhain, I stayed busy
preparing for the celebration and tried not to focus
solely on Banquo's return. Uald and I arranged rocks
around the center cauldron in the shape of a star. We
then banked up five fires at each of the star's points.
Aridmis and I collected gourds, acorns, and late fall
herbs to adorn the tables. The others were busy as well.
In preparation for the event, Druanne and Sid had gone
to prepare a special elixir that would loosen the spirit
and allow us to interact with our ancestors.

"The elixir of the ancestors is a heavy potion.
Druanne must fast and pray in order to prepare it
properly. She and Sid have journeyed to a sacred place
to prepare the draft," Epona told me when I'd gone
looking for Sid.

"The mound?" I asked.

Epona shook her head. "There are many sacred
places nearby. You will learn them all, in time."

I frowned. I didn't like the idea of Druanne and Sid together. I knew Sid would watch over Druanne, would keep her safe, but who would watch over Sid? The thought of the two of them together made me feel nauseated. As I waited, I also worked alongside Bride, who had been repairing and making new ceremonial masks.

One evening before Samhain, I sat working in Bride's small house. Her home had two small bedrooms, one reserved for the mysterious Tully who I had not yet met, set off from a main sitting room where we worked in front of a stone fireplace. Her room was adorned with dried flowers and framed embroidery. It was warm and clean and smelled like milled soap. Bride had unbraided her long, gray hair and let it fall freely all around her. She looked lovely, but ancient, in the firelight. Her lined face wrinkled like ripples on the water.

"When the moon rises, we will all wear our masks so the gods may come more freely amongst us, and the Samhain potion will loosen our spirits. The dead will wander freely amongst the living. You never know who you will see, my dear," she said as she handed me one of the completed masks, "but I know the last person I want to see is my late husband!" she added with a laugh which I joined.

"You suppose old MacAlpin will visit me?" I asked jokingly.

Bride smiled and shook her head. "We both best be careful whose names we whisper on the wind. After all, you keep what you conjure," Bride said, then looked thoughtful. "Maybe I'll see that young buck who lifted my skirts on Beltane eve when I was fifteen, if he's on the other side," she said, then laughed again. "He had such lovely eyes, lovely skin. In fact, he looked a bit like your druid." Bride winked at me.

My druid. I grinned at her then studied the stag mask I held in my hands. Half of the mask had been made from the skull of a stag, its antlers still intact. It had been sewn onto a pelt so it might be worn over the head. Small bells and feathers had been strung to the antlers. I set the mask into the basket with the others. Within, I saw that Bride had made a mask with black raven feathers. I lifted the mask. She had shaped the leather so the face looked like a beak.

Bride smiled. "I made that one for you."

"Thank you," I said, lifting the mask to my face. It touched me that she had made something for me in particular, a gift for the new me. I looked out the eye-slits. I was struck with a strange, dizzying sensation.

"Not yet," Bride said, gently taking the mask from my hands. "It may look simple enough, but every stitch is a spell. It is the craft of the Crone," she said with a grin, her blue eyes twinkling. "One day you will learn," she added then set the mask into the basket with the others, "when you are gray like this old hare," she added with a chuckle.

ON SAMHAIN EVE MORNING, THE jingling of rigging woke me. With no regard to the tangle my hair had become nor the fact that I was still wearing my bed clothes, I jumped from bed and ran to the coven square:

Banquo had come. My heart pounded in my chest. Finally, he had returned.

"Merry met!" I called to Banquo and Balor.

Balor smiled as he removed the red hood he was wearing, uncovering his bald head. "Blessed Samhain to you, Lady Cerridwen."

"And to you, Wise Father," I replied, but my eyes had already turned to Banquo. I fought back tears of joy.

Banquo dismounted and rushed to me, catching me up in his arms. "My dear," he whispered in my ear, kissing me on the cheek.

Behind me, the door to Epona's house opened. I didn't see her, but I could feel her behind me. She cleared her throat.

Banquo set me down. Blushing, he turned and bowed respectfully to her. "My Lady," he said, "may the Old Ones smile on you."

She laughed good-naturedly then clapped him on the shoulder. "Dear Banquo. May your ancestors bless you on this holy day." She then gave Banquo an odd look, the expression looking like something between curiosity and sympathy, and I wondered why. Was she unhappy with the relationship that had grown between us or did she know something?

I didn't care. It was Samhain eve, the night when the dead walked, and Banquo and I were together again. It was the holiday that marked the new year for those who celebrated the old ways. The harvest done, the Goddess would begin her winter slumber.

Aridmis emerged from her cabin to welcome Balor and Banquo, and Uald stuck her head out of the smithy.

"Cerridwen," Uald called. "You and Banquo can come help me."

Banquo and I crossed the square while casting nervous glances at one another. My stomach was full of butterflies. I felt so happy but also uneasy. Had Banquo talked to his father? Did he have any news? Would he be angry to learn I had nothing to tell him? Would he wait longer? My mind was filled with a thousand questions and worries.

"Are you all right?" Banquo asked. "When you sent the casting, I worried."

I smiled at him. "I just missed you desperately."

"I'm glad I was able to make it in time. I nearly had to enchant Lord Thorfinn in order to get him to release me. But he is a romantic. When I told him I traveled to see my love, he let me go."

I squeezed Banquo's hand, but remembering Madelaine's words about Thorfinn, my mind spun with a flurry of questions. "A romantic, eh? Is Thorfinn wed? In love?"

"He's mad for a girl from Norway, doing anything he can to win her hand. He's almost as mad as I am for you."

We stopped at the gate of the smithy. Uald was in the barn.

Banquo leaned in and kissed me quickly. I reached up and touched his face. His beard was filling out. It looked handsome on him and was long enough that it felt soft to the touch. I gazed into his chestnut-colored eyes.

"Later...let's talk?" Banquo asked.

I nodded just as Uald came around the corner of the smithy. She stood with her hands on her hips, a bemused expression on her face. I noticed then that she was dressed for hunting. Her hair was pulled up into a braided bun at the back of head, her bow strung on her back.

"Well, did I give you enough time?" she asked.

I winked at her. "No."

"Sorry," she said with a laugh. "Hurry it up a bit next time. Let's go."

"Go?" Banquo asked.

"I'm headed out to check my traps. We need game for tonight's celebration. The ancestors will be hungry. But if you'd rather stay…" she said, looking behind us.

Banquo and I turned. Balor, Epona, Aridmis, and Bride had already gathering in a circle to begin what Sid had forewarned me would be a long day of prayer.

"Lead the way," Banquo said, and soon we were following Uald into the forest.

Kelpie and the other horses nickered at us as we passed the pen into the woods. Soon, we were deep in the woods. Most of the trees had lost their leaves. The bright autumn hues of orange and red had faded to dull brown. It was cold at night, and in the morning, the first frosts froze the grasses, making them brittle. The loamy scent of the decay of fall had started to fade, replaced by the nose-chilling wind and the threat of snow.

Uald led us to an area in the woods where I'd never traveled before. Here, the trees were massive. The last leaves clung to the branches, twisting like bats hanging from the limbs.

"A moment," Banquo called as we passed under an ancient oak tree. He pulled a small golden sickle from his belt, stuck it between his teeth, then grabbed a limb and pulled himself up into the tree. "Mistletoe," he explained through clenched teeth.

As he pulled himself up, his tunic lifted, and I saw the line of dark hair trailing down his muscular stomach and below his waistline. My body tingled as I thought about that day at the spring and the feel of his hands. Banquo easily pulled himself up into the tree.

"Cut a bundle for me as well," Uald called up to him.

We stood under the tree and watched as Banquo moved adeptly amongst the limbs harvesting the herb. For the druids, mistletoe was one of the most sacred of all herbs.

"He is nice to look at," Uald said. She cocked her hip and grinned as she looked at Banquo, her lips pulling to one side.

"I thought you didn't care for romantic nonsense," I teased.

"I'm not being romantic. He's just nice to look at. But I do like him. I hope it ends well for you."

Madelaine. Madelaine, where are you? I thought. How could I explain to Banquo? I still wasn't sure what I was going to say. I knew, without a doubt, that Banquo and I belonged together. But I still could not tell him who I was for risk of losing it all.

Banquo jumped from the branches and landed with a grunt, righting himself at once. He handed a clutch of mistletoe to Uald who nodded to him in thanks, stuck the herb into her game sack and headed back into the forest.

"I was surprised to see you," Banquo told me when Uald was a good distance ahead of us.

"The casting?"

He nodded.

"Sid is teaching me to control my power."

"You once mentioned that you too have walked in the forgotten spaces."

I nodded.

"Where did you go?"

For a moment, I thought of the Wyrd Sisters. I had not seen them in so long. Perhaps they were done with me. "I'm not exactly sure," I said with a shake of the head.

"Once I—" Banquo began.

"Here," Uald called.

We hurried up to Uald who was standing over a trap where a small hare struggled to get free. Uald motioned for me to open up the bag. Grabbing the hare with her gloves hands, she snapped the creature's neck then tossed him in the bag.

My mind drifted, dreaming of the taste of roasted rabbit. I hadn't eaten since the evening before. I was starving. The fast had me feeling dizzy. But of course, this flesh was not for me. Tonight we would serve our ancestors. We would welcome them back to the realm of the living, offer them a feast, and pray for their guidance. It was Samhain eve. Tonight, the dead would walk.

After we emptied Uald's traps, we started back toward the coven. Then suddenly Uald stopped.

"Nine Ash," Uald said as she pointed west. "Follow nine ash trees. They will lead you home. I have something I need to take care of. You'll reach the coven in about half an hour…or so," she said with a wink then left us alone. She disappeared into the trees, whistling as she wandered away from us.

"Where is she going?" Banquo wondered aloud.

I suspected she was headed to check on Druanne and Sid, but I didn't say so. It was not my place to divulge my sister's secrets. And I also suspected Uald had formulated this plan just to give us this time alone. I was grateful to her.

Despite the chill in the air, the long walk had made me hot. I was parched and my head hurt, but Epona had forbidden us to drink. "Can we rest a bit?" I asked Banquo, motioning to a boulder near the first ash tree.

He nodded then joined me on the rock. I rubbed my eyes and stretched out my long legs.

"So you missed me?" Banquo asked with a teasing smile as he took my hand, "my lady with the violet eyes." He touched my chin gently.

"Enough to jump out of my skin for you!"

He laughed. "Then it must be love. I certainly haven't had a woman do that for me before. But then again, I've never met anyone quite like you."

I smiled softly at him.

He leaned in and gently kissed my lips. "Sweet priestess of the cauldron," he whispered. "I did stop in Lochaber when I travelled north. My father…he wants me to serve alongside Jarl Thorfinn for a year before he will hear of any marriage. But he did say, perhaps, if he knew more about the lady he could be convinced otherwise. He wasn't keen on the mystery of your identity, though Balor vouched for your lineage without divulging details. It seems my master knows who you are. And your aunt, did she…?"

"I spoke to her and pled our case. We have a male relative—my uncle—who must decide. Ultimately, it is for him to say. I haven't heard from my aunt. I don't know my uncle's decision on the matter yet."

"Cerridwen," he said looking closely at me, "Lochaber is a vast holding. Surely, I am a good match for you."

I sucked in my bottom lip, chewing on it as anxiety wracked my stomach and made my already pounding head feel worse. What could I say? He was right. For just about any girl in the land, he was a great match, and he loved me. And I loved him. "You, my love, are the only match for me," I said, leaning in to kiss his sweet lips. I caught the scents of rosemary and mint in his hair. I inhaled deeply, trying to draw in his very essence.

Banquo pulled me toward him and began to kiss me passionately. I wrapped my arms around him and held him tight. He slid from the boulder and came to sit on his knees in front of me, between my legs, clutching me about the waist. He buried his face against my chest. "I love you. Please, tell me who you are," he whispered.

The words nearly tumbled from my mouth, but I bit them back. He was asking for the hand of Boite's daughter. Without knowing it, he was positioning himself so his sons would have a claim to the throne of Scotland. What would he think, what would he do, when he knew who I really was? Would he fear to aim so high? Would he flee from me out of hopelessness? Would he divulge it too soon to those who would make decisions for us? I didn't want to lose him. Maybe

Madelaine could convince Malcolm. I had to let her try. If she succeeded, Lochaber would win a great prize. And if Madelaine was not successful, Lochaber's bid was just one out of many, and no one would begrudge him. It was not impossible that if he knew who I really was, he might leave me, knowing it could never be. I couldn't take the sting of it, not yet, not while there was still hope.

"I'm Cerridwen," I whispered. In the end, I was hiding my bloodline while admitting the truth of my soul. My kin could cost me his love, but my soul belonged to him.

Banquo stood, kissed me on the forehead, and held out his hand. He looked pale, his mouth turning sadly. "Let's go back," he said. We walked silently back through the forest. I bit back tears. I knew I had hurt him, and it wounded me terribly. But there was no way I could make him understand, at least not yet. I was so sorry. I wanted to explain everything to him, but I couldn't. I was afraid. The whole way back to the coven I wrestled with the problem, but never found the right words to make him understand. I loved him. I loved him so much. I chewed on my lip and tried not to cry, all the while cursing the blood in my veins.

By the time we had returned, the bards had arrived.

"Lady Cerridwen and Lord Banquo," Bergen, the leader of the bards, called when we emerged from the woods. It was almost as if he was announcing us at court, like a married couple. I felt the sting of it.

"My brothers," Banquo called cheerfully, pulling on a false face, then he turned to me. "My love, do you mind?" he asked me softly, motioning to the bards. His face looked haunted, his eyes watery.

"Banquo," I whispered and reached up and touched his cheek. He closed his eyes when my hand rested on his skin. "I love you. Please know how much I love you."

He smiled, took my hand, and kissed my fingers. "I trust you," he whispered then pressed my hand against his lips. "And I love you too." Once more, he kissed me on the forehead then went to welcome the bards.

I scanned the group. Sigurd was not there.

"My Lady," Brant called to me as he led the horses to the watering trough. "Fasting makes you even more beautiful! Your skin is glowing like the moon!"

"What can I say? I am a dark goddess," I replied, grateful to have a distraction. My stomach felt sick. It was too horrible to feel Banquo's hurt and frustration. I didn't know what to do. At the risk of losing him, I didn't speak. By not speaking, I risked losing him.

"Then it is your night. Let's see who seeks you from the other side!"

I smiled. Whichever of my ancestors would walk that night, I hoped, at least they would come with some guidance. Because, once again, I felt to my core that I was an orphan.

We spent most of the day in silent prayer or busying preparing the feasting table. Once Uald returned, I worked as much as I could with her; she seemed adept at avoiding Epona's ministering. Epona and Uald, old friends, functioned in many ways like equals. And, I noticed, Epona was more apt to let me slide when Uald had a good reason for me to do so. Uald was also very astute, and she picked up on the distance between Banquo and me.

"Are you all right?" she whispered as we sat in the smithy skinning hares.

I nodded, working a knife just under the skin of the hare, a trick Uald herself had taught me. I shot a glance over my shoulder at Banquo who was sitting in silent prayer near the center cauldron.

"I haven't told him who I am, my family. He wants to wed me, but he needs to know who I am. Who I really am."

"Of course. They won't marry Lochaber's heir to just any girl."

I nodded. "When he reaches for me, he reaches—"

"For Scotland, without knowing it," she finished my sentence. "Do you love him?"

"With all my heart. I *know* him, Uald. As sure as I know myself."

Uald threw a pile of guts into a slop bucket. Her knife got away from her, dropping into the pail. I reached down to get it for her. But when I pulled my hands back, they were completely covered in blood and bits.

"Ugh," Uald groaned. She grabbed my hands and tried to wipe the blood away. The more she tried to clean the sticky liquid, the more it spread. "Out, damned spot! Out, I say," she cursed jokingly.

I stared at my hands. Blood dripped from my fingers. I swooned. All at once, the images started to get mixed up, and I fell into a vision of myself on a battlefield. Blood, lots and lots of blood, dripped down my hands and arms. My whole body shook. Mist swirled around me. I could hear men nearby, but they were lost in the fog. A corpse chopped to bits lay on the field below me. I looked up; I was holding a heart, its blood emptying all over me, in my raised hands. In my vision, I screamed loudly, triumphantly, then cried out Banquo's name. Hearing his name knocked me from the vision.

I stood with a start, bumping the stool out from under me. The half-skinned hare dropped to the ground. The image of the hare's carcass overlapped in my mind with the image of the bloody dead body I'd seen in my vision. I shut my eyes and squeezed them tightly, trying to force the gruesome image away.

"Corbie?" Uald asked, so startled she'd dropped my goddess name, grabbing me and holding me steady.

"Cerridwen!" Banquo jumped the smithy wall and took me from Uald's hands, holding me firmly but tenderly. "Are you all right?"

"A vision," I whispered, trembling.

Aridmis rushed up behind Banquo. "Cerridwen?" she called. Worry wracked her usually placid face.

"She had a vision," Uald whispered. "The blood."

"I've got her." Aridmis took me gently by the arm. "Don't be alarmed. It's the nature of Samhain, a night where blood is sacred. It draws out the images, the past and future existing all at once with the present." She led me back to the fire.

Silent, Banquo walked alongside us, his arm wrapped around my waist.

Aridmis sat me down near the cauldron then wetted a cloth. She pulled a vial of lavender oil from her satchel and sweetened the fabric. "What did you see?" she asked as she cleaned my hands.

"So much blood," I whispered. I was still shaking. I wasn't sure if what I saw was a memory of the past or a vision of the future. It terrified me.

Aridmis looked at Banquo and me as she worked on my hands. "It is no mistake you called his name," she told me then cast a glance at Banquo. "I have spun the wheel and looked into your future. As you have always been, the two of you are one, but heed my words. In this life, your love will bring an end to one of you. I cannot see who. The tie between you is the strongest bond I have ever seen. It glows like a silver light from one of you to the other. But this love will end in blood." Aridmis stood. "I'm sorry," she said then left us to stare at one another dumbfounded.

Banquo put his arm around me. "Don't fear," he whispered. "Tonight, we will put it before the ancestors and let them decide." His words were mysterious, and I was too shaken to puzzle it out. I bit my lip, closed my eyes, and rested my head on his shoulder. In that moment, all I wanted to feel was the present.

twenty-one

IT WAS SUNDOWN WHEN DRUANNE finally emerged from the forest. She wore long, black robes and carried a vial of red liquid and a small wooden goblet. Her face looked very pale, and her eyes had a faraway look. Her arrival marked the beginning of the night's ritual.

"Where's Sid?" I whispered to Uald who was standing beside me. I had recovered from the vision the blood had prompted earlier that day, but Aridmis' words and the tenor of the day left me feeling shaky and on edge. It was as if I could feel the worlds thinning between us as we moved toward midnight. What was real, what was past, what was present, all were starting to get confused. I hated the feeling.

"Gone."

My stomach dropped, churning with worry. "Gone where?"

Uald shrugged.

We gathered at the center of the coven, standing in a circle around the star we had laid with stone, the five fires at each point, the center cauldron fire burning brightly. Druanne came to stand in the middle. Once she was in place, we began.

"Once the wheel has gone round," Druanne called.

"Once again the year has come and gone," Balor echoed.

"And with time, we too shall fade. And with time, we too shall die," Epona called.

Her words chilled me. I glanced sidelong at Banquo. What did Aridmis mean that our love would result in one of our deaths? Was she right?

"But not this night," Druanne answered.

"This night we live and bid you spirits rise," Bride called.

"By the Morrigu, by Scotia, by the Crone, join our feast," I called.

Banquo spoke next. "Ancient ones, cross the divide. Join us on this night."

"In peace," Bergen called out, striking a cord on his harp. The discordant sound carried across the night's sky.

"In goodwill," Ivar the bard added then began beating his drum rhythmically.

"With our thanks," Druanne called.

"So mote it be," Balor intoned.

"So mote it be," we all answered.

As Ivar continued to beat his drum, Druanne began her progression. One by one, she went to each person and offered them a drink of the potion, whispering something in their ear. After, everyone stood in quiet contemplation. I saw Aridmis swoon, struggling to keep her footing. Behind Druanne, Bride followed with her basket of masks. Epona donned a mask with long silver and red horsehair, the face made from a horse's skull. Seeing her like that made me shiver.

A moment later, Druanne stepped in front of me, blocking my view. I was surprised to see how... changed...she looked. Her eyes were very distant. Her skin was pale, the blue veins on her forehead protruding. She looked almost ethereal.

"Blood of MacAlpin," she whispered in my ear. "Honor your ancestors," she said, handing the potion to me. Her voice sounded hollow.

Her hand was shaking as she held out a small wood cup full of the potion. I drank the sharp liquid then handed the cup back to her. It tasted bitter; my tongue caught the taste of mushrooms, berries, and acorns. There were other sharp, herbal tastes. When the liquid hit my stomach, I almost vomited. Taking a deep breath, I held the liquid down.

With a smile, Bride handed me the raven mask. "Now, my sweet girl," she whispered.

I pulled the mask on, again hit with that same dizzying sensation. I stared out through the slits in the eyes, and this time my vision seemed sharper. I felt like I could see from far away. I looked at Ivar who had, at some point, put on some odd mask formed from a bear's skin. I blinked, and it seemed then truly to be a bear standing in his place.

Once everyone had drunk the potion and donned their masks, we all walked around the circle counterclockwise, meeting again at the feasting table.

Epona stood at the head of the table. Silently, we all stood behind one chair at the table. Banquo stood across from me. He was wearing the stag mask, looking out at me through the socket's in the stag's skull.

"We call you, ancestors. The walls between the worlds are thin tonight. Join us from the beyond. Dine and dance with us this night. Come amongst us. Take pleasure in these earthly things. Whisper your secrets and feel our love," Epona called.

"Call your ancestors!" Balor ordered.

"Thomas," Epona called.

"Aiden," Bride called.

"Dorrit," Uald called.

They went around until they came to me. "Emer!"

"Brighid," Banquo called. His sister, I guessed.

Once we'd all evoked our ancestors, Balor called out, "Ancestors, you are welcome. Eat! Dance and be merry so they may remember the feel of flesh and the pleasure of life!"

With that, we all filled the plates before us, not to eat, but to serve. I never knew my mother. I had no idea what she liked to eat. I knew nothing about her. Feeling miserable, I set her plate and poured her a glass of honey mead not knowing if she would have preferred ale or wine. Behind my mask, tears streamed down my face. In the end, my mother was a stranger to me. She would never come. I felt alone in my misery.

"Come, my dear," I heard Bride say, putting her soft hand in mine. She wore a dark mask that covered her face with black lace. She led me to the fires where the bards had pulled out their instruments and joined Ivar, who was still drumming, in making wild music. I scanned around for Banquo. He was gone. Aridmis and Epona began to dance. The place shimmered with glowing orbs of silver and while light.

I felt hot and very dizzy. The entire world spun. I looked out with the raven's eyes and my vision doubled. The music clanged strangely. Everyone looked deformed in their masks. And suddenly, the coven seemed to be full of people. I sensed a great number of spirits lurking there with us. Intermixed in the crowd, I swore I could see the smiling faces of maidens, Priestesses and Druids, who'd come before us. Their clothes, from courtly dresses to animal skins, hinted at ages past. The dead, our ancestors, had heard our call. For a glimmering moment, I saw Epona standing face to face with the shining spirit of a young, handsome man. Her wild boy. Their eyes were locked on one another. Had his name been Thomas? Was that who she'd called?

And then I felt someone very close to me. I turned to look for Banquo, but it wasn't him. A woman had touched me gently then turned and walked away from me toward the forest. I squinted with my raven eyes and studied her. She hand long, daffodil-colored hair and green robes. Emer. She turned and smiled at me, beckoning me to follow her. Like a fey thing, she floated over ferns and fallen logs deeper into the forest on feet that never touched the ground.

"Mother?" I called after her.

She turned and smiled at me but didn't stop. She beckoned me forward, leading me deep into the forest. I moved swiftly after her. I prayed she would stop, would talk to me. I would have given anything to hear just one word from her. I desperately wanted to look at her face. My mother had come. I rushed deeper into the woods, following her. We passed through a thick stand of trees and came to a clearing. At the center of the clearing, bathed in moonlight, stood my druid.

My mother stopped at the edge of the clearing. I moved toward them, stopping as I neared my mother's shade. My heart felt like it was shattering in half. I looked into her face, into her eyes. She shimmered. Her eyes were so green! I had never known that, that her eyes were the color of new leaves in spring. She smiled at me, raising one heavy brow at me, then smirked playfully.

"Mother?" I whispered, but she shook her head, motioning with her fingers to her lips that she could not speak. She smiled at me gently then flourished her hand toward Banquo. I turned and looked at him.

My druid. My bridegroom. My love. My husband. He was everything to me.

I took two steps toward him but turned and looked back at my mother. She nodded to me then turned and floated back into the forest. Not far away, waiting on a small knoll, was my father. My mother went to him and took his hand then the pair faded back into the ether. I turned back toward Banquo.

Behind the raven mask, my vision was still in double. The world around me glowed with the silver light of the moon. Banquo motioned for me to follow him then began walking through the trees.

"Where are we going?" I tried to ask him, but I swore that instead of my voice, I heard the caw of a raven.

Banquo looked back at me, but he was not himself. He was a stag, strong and powerful, his wide horns glimmering in the moonlight. He was no longer a man, he'd become the embodiment of the horned god. He had morphed into his true form. And as I moved, I realized that I was no longer myself either. I followed him on my raven's wings. I too had revealed my true nature. I was the embodiment of my clan's crest. I was Cerridwen, but I was also a MacAlpin: I was the daughter of ravens.

I followed my stag deeper into the forest. Soon we came to a giant oak tree at the center of a grove I did not recognize. The tree was immense and seemed as old as the woods itself. How was it I had never seen this tree before? I looked around me and realized that nothing looked familiar anymore. I wasn't near the coven. I had walked...no, I had flown...between the worlds. I scanned all around. In the darkness just beyond the tree, tall Samhain fires burned. I saw silhouettes of men and women spinning fire. They held long torches, flames burning at the ends, and spun the flames, making ancient shapes appear on the canvas of night. From somewhere in the dark, I heard the beating of drums and the sound of flute music.

"Where are we?" I asked Banquo who stood before me still in the form of a stag. This time, however, I heard my voice. And moments after I spoke, I felt a shift in myself. My raven wings had gone.

Banquo turned and looked at me, morphing from a stag to a man. He took my hand. "Lost in time."

I peered around me, trying to make out the people nearby. I saw their woad-painted faces and primal clothes. Their hair was braided in a strange fashion, and they beat on shields made of leather. They carried copper swords, and the bards amongst them played flutes made of bone. They were the Picts, the ancient blood of Alba. We had traveled back, or perhaps we had been conjured back, in time.

I stared at Banquo and then I knew the truth. Banquo had led me to one of the thin places. We had not traveled back in time: we had simply found a place where all times exist. He had taken me between the worlds, to a place stuck in the very middle.

Banquo reached toward me and pulled off my mask. Tentatively, I too reached up and removed his. With the masks off, Bride's spells were undone. Some of the dizziness passed. Druanne's potion, however, still had my mind reeling. Regardless, we were, once more, Cerridwen and Banquo. And in that moment, all of the chaos and noise and fire and people simply faded. The ancestors departed. The forest became still and quiet. There was no one and nothing but us and the moon. We stood alone under a tall oak tree in the forest in the dark of night.

"Marry me, my love. Here, in this old, sacred place, before the Gods and our ancestors, marry me," Banquo said then.

I stared at him.

"Maybe our family will deny us in the end, so marry me here, as my priestess and I am your druid. Marry me here as Cerridwen. And as Cerridwen, you are my wife, my bride. Before your ancestors and mine, marry me. Before the old gods, please, Cerridwen."

"Yes." I knelt down on the mossy ground at the foot of the oak tree. Taking Banquo's hand, I pulled him down to join me. My druid then pulled out his ceremonial, silver-hilted knife. I wasn't surprise to see it was capped with a stag's head.

"By the Father God," he said, "Stag Lord Cernunnos of the Forest…"

"And by the Great Mother, as Maiden, Mother, and Crone…"

"I pledge my soul, my heart, and my blood to you," Banquo said.

With a quick move, Banquo ran his hand along the top of the blade. Sharp crimson erupted from his flesh, blood pooling in his hand.

"And I pledge my soul, my heart, and my blood to you," I told him. I took his knife and sliced my hand the same way Banquo had done. The metal bit sharply. The pain seared my palm, shooting pain all the way to my shoulder. I shuddered but accepted it. The sacrifice of blood would bind us, no matter what fate threw in our way. I was pledging myself to him, to my druid, with my blood and my soul. There was no deeper bond. This was the old way of marrying, bonding our spirits together. My guess was that this was not the first time we had performed such a ritual. No matter what, Banquo and I would always be connected. And beyond all imagining, my mother had been the one to bless my marriage.

We joined our hands together, our blood mingling. The essence of our beings mixed together. I closed my eyes. The cut throbbed. I felt the warmth of Banquo's hand, his blood wet against my palm, my fingers.

"You are mine," Banquo whispered. "And I am yours."

"You are mine, and I am yours," I replied. "Bound through time."

"From life to life."

We leaned in and kissed one another.

"No matter what happens, we are linked as man and wife, priest and priestess, before the gods," Banquo whispered in my ear.

"So mote it be," I whispered in reply.

Banquo kissed me gently then lay me back on the forest floor. Above me, I saw the tall limbs of the oak tree stretching into the night's sky, the moon high and full above us. I kissed my husband desperately. I tasted the potion on his mouth, the sharp tang of mushroom and herbs on his lips. I smelled his skin and tasted the sweat on his neck. Though the air was cool, I pulled off his shirt. I wanted to see him. His chest was tattooed with swirling designs, old symbols that pledged his undying allegiance to the old gods. I stroked my hand across his skin, feeling the hair on his chest.

"Land and sea," I whispered then pulled off my dress and undergarments.

Banquo undid his pants. "Forever one," Banquo replied. He pulled me up and toward him, kissing me hard, then lay me back down on the ground. I felt the bare earth beneath me. Its energy rose from the ground and filled my spirit. Banquo kissed my face, my neck, my breasts. He opened my legs and soon I felt his wet mouth below, making me tremble. He then rose, and I reached out to stroke him.

"I'll be easy," he whispered in my ear, and moments later I felt his cock press into me. I felt the sting as my maidenhood tore for him. I whimpered a little, and

Banquo moved easily, carefully. "I love you," he whispered in my ear.

As he moved, the pain faded. We locked our eyes on one another. His curly hair became wet with sweat and stuck to his forehead. His eyes were soft and loving. He leaned down and kissed me again and again. I loved the feel of him inside me. I closed my eyes and stretched my arms out on the ground, feeling the leaves and earth under me. I looked up at the moon. Everything around me was alive with magic.

I wrapped my legs around Banquo and moved in tandem with him, feeling my body rising in passion. Banquo began to breathe hard. I was sweating with him. My body began to shake with pleasure, a feeling like lightning shooting from my head to my toes as I felt Banquo inside me, growing larger, moving faster, until he found release.

Exhausted, we both lay still on the ground, Banquo still inside me.

"My Priestess," he whispered. "My bride."

It was the last thing I heard before I fell asleep.

I WOKE THE NEXT MORNING to find the forest covered in thick fog. I could barely see an arm's length in front of me. Banquo was gone and so were my clothes.

"Banquo?" I called in a whisper. My voice echoed in the mist. "Banquo?"

There was no answer, but I heard the sound of a small hammer striking an anvil somewhere in the distance. Uald?

I sighed. Where had Banquo gone? And how had I managed to lose my clothes? I headed toward the smithy, prepping myself for all the jokes I knew Uald would make. But I had given myself on my own terms. I had wed the man of my choice. It was done now, no matter what anyone said. Now I would be the bride of the son of Lochaber.

I moved forward in the fog, following the sound of the small hammer. I stepped carefully. I was not certain where Banquo had led me, but surely it was somewhere near the smithy. I just must not have noticed the tree before. Perhaps Balor had shown Banquo the place. Druids, after all, were oak seekers.

Soon the outline of the smithy started to clear. I walked toward it but got confused. It didn't look quite like Uald's smithy.

I saw the shape of someone standing near the anvil. They stopped and turned to look toward me. I took two more steps in the fog as it swirled around me. Across from me, the other person took a few steps toward me. Moments later, I was standing across from the black-haired man from my visions. He was wearing a leather smith's apron but was shirtless underneath; sweat rolled down his neck. He was very fair. He had skin white as snow, his eyes clear and bright blue. In one hand, he held a small hammer, in the other, a shield he had been crafting. On it he had pounded the symbol of a raven.

"You!" he whispered then stepped toward me.

I opened my mouth to speak, not even sure what I would say, but all I heard was a raven's shriek.

I sat up with a start.

"Are you all right?" Banquo whispered, sitting up beside me. "Heavy mist," he said then, pulling me back down beside him. He covered us with his tunic. "Balor says to never sleep in the fog...too dangerous. The worlds are too thin at such times," he said sleepily. "But you are so warm, and my head is still so heavy," he said, snuggling close to me, "wife" he added with a chuckle. He closed his eyes and slept again, leaving me alone and shaking.

twenty-two

Banquo and I returned early in the morning before the others woke. The pentacle fires had burned out but the coals under the center cauldron were still glowing red. Quietly, I led Banquo into my little house where Thora was sleeping on what used to be Ludmilla's bed. She raised her head and looked at us when we entered then rolled on her back and went back to sleep.

"Get warm," I whispered to Banquo, motioning to my bed. The air had cooled overnight, and we'd woken on the cold, frozen ground. After my…vision…my sleep had been restless. I was woken over and over again by strange, bloody nightmares. The dreams featured people I didn't know, rain, fire, and blood. And my raven-haired man was at the center of it all. Who was he? I shuddered just thinking about it.

"You're trembling," Banquo whispered, pulling me onto the bed beside him. "You're not afraid, are you? Your aunt…"

I shook my head as I nestled into his arms, pulling the covers up to my chin. It wasn't the real world that frightened me. "No, only cold. I love you, and my mother's spirit led me to you. I have no doubts in my mind."

Banquo kissed my shoulder. "Balor and I will ride north again this morning. I have to rejoin Jarl Thorfinn. Once you talk to you aunt, just send word. I'll make the arrangements to have you join me. You'll like Jarl Thorfinn. He's got a kind spirit. He's like a brother to me."

"Then Lochaber promotes Thorfinn's bid for power?" I asked nervously. If Banquo's family was allied against mine, then I would have no choice but to abandon Madelaine and Malcolm. I would have to turn on my blood, throw my allegiance behind the north, just to keep my husband. It was an act that could cost me my head, but my choice had already been made. I had given my heart.

"Lochaber favors Thorfinn and Macbeth as the rightful powers in the north, but we are not interested in waging war…at least not yet. My father is waiting to see how the King will play out the game now that Gillacoemgain of Moray has usurped power by killing Macbeth's father, Findelach. No one knows for certain why King Malcolm plotted against his own daughter's husband, but Findelach is dead. Macbeth's claim is weakened. One thing is for certain, the path to the throne is much less complicated for King Malcolm's favorite, Duncan. Cerridwen, my father's allegiances…do they complicate things for you?"

More than he could ever know. "No," I said then. "You are my husband now. The matter is no longer complicated." And in my heart, I told myself that I really believed it.

BANQUO AND I DIDN'T SPEAK a word of our marriage to anyone. And he was right, as soon as Balor had risen, he roused Banquo and bid him say his goodbyes. I followed my husband around the coven like a sick, miserable thing. No matter how hungry I had felt the day before, now my stomach tossed and turned with anxiety. Maybe the potion of the ancestors had pushed us beyond where our logic would have allowed us to go, but we loved each other. My mother had led me to my druid. I had wed him before the old gods. That's all there was to it.

"We will not be back until spring," I heard Balor tell Epona. She held the reins to his horse while he mounted.

"May the great ones watch over you. The winter will be long and harsh. Take care," she told him, kissing his hand in respect.

I turned my attention to Banquo. "I'll send word soon," I whispered, handing him his reins. Hot tears were streaming down my cheeks. My heart ached.

"As soon as you can," Banquo said. His eyes were watery. "I hate this."

"It will be done soon," I reassured him.

He leaned over and kissed me on my head. "Let it be done then. Come to me in Caithness. Let's make babies all winter," he said then laughed.

In spite of myself, I chuckled and wiped the tears from my cheeks.

Balor reined his horse in and motioned for Banquo to follow. With a wave, my husband rode off leaving me amongst my sisters. I watched him go, studying every inch of his body. I tried to memorize his frame. I tried to remember his taste and the feel of his hands. I etched his image in my mind. And once more, before he passed through the wall sheltering our grove, he turned and looked back at me. And in that moment, I felt my heart break.

I DECIDED I WOULD WAIT until night to tell Epona everything. The bards weren't planning to leave until later that afternoon. I stayed inside my little house most of the day and thought over what I would say to Epona, to Madelaine. In my mind, the matter was final. It didn't matter what Malcolm wanted. He could marry someone else to Duncan, or Thorfinn, or anyone else for all I cared. I was married to Banquo.

The moon was high in the sky when I finally went to seek Epona. The coven was dark. All the women had gone to bed. Smoke rolled out of the little chimneys. It would be hard to tell Epona that I was leaving, and I would need to send a casting to Madelaine. It had to be done. I wouldn't keep anymore secrets from Banquo. I would send the casting and be done with it. As I headed across the square, I noticed smoke trailing from Sid's house. I looked at Epona's door. It could wait a few more minutes. Surely, Sid could advise me.

I stopped at the center fire on my way to Sid's. No doubt she hadn't eaten. Small pots sat warming on stones all around the cauldron. Aridmis had made lamb mutton. I could still smell its sweet scent. I bent beside the fire.

The bank of coals under the cauldron flickered like a beating heart, thumping red, orange, and black. It had grown very cold outside. I could smell the threat of snow in the air. I was about to lift one of the pot lids when I saw a shadow out of the corner of my eye. In the hours waning from Samhain, it did not pay to ignore shades. The dead, especially those who did not wish to be dead, still roamed the land. And they were not all friendly.

I stood to find a woman standing a few feet back from the fire. She was half-concealed by shadows, but I could still make out her features. Her hair was scarlet red, the color of velvet and blood. Her locks were twisted over her shoulder, decorated with black gems and small bones. She held a tall staff topped with a human skull, and on her left shoulder sat a raven.

"My Lady," I whispered, bowing my head. My knees went soft. A sharp pain spread across my chest as wild panic beat through my veins. Why had the Goddess of Death come?

"Do you know who I am?" she asked, and I realized then that she sounded angry.

"You...you are the Morrigu," I stammered, looking up at her.

She smiled, her lips curling to reveal sharp, pointed teeth. "I am death."

"Pray, what service can I offer you, Lady?" I whispered.

She laughed a full-blooded laugh. "Prey," she said then paused. "I have marked you as mine since your birth. It was me who answered Boite's call. The time has come for you to do my will."

My whole body shook. My heart beat so hard I could hear it slamming in my chest, my eardrums throbbing. "I am yours to command."

"It is time to join your sisters of the cauldron."

"The cauldron...the Wyrds?"

The Morrigu clenched her jaw. I could feel anger emanating from her. Her eyes narrowed. She took a step toward me. "Did you think your destiny was your own to choose? Saucy and over-bold, how dare you traffic and trade with Banquo in riddles and the affairs of men, giving what was not yours to give? You don't belong to Malcolm or Madelaine or Banquo or even yourself. I am your mistress. Boite gave you to me. I am the source of all that power locked inside you. You...are mine. And you will go where I command. You will learn what I deem fitting when I decide."

"I—" I began, but I wasn't sure to what to say. My knees were shaking.

The Morrigu nodded to her raven. It flew to Epona's window to peck on the glass.

"I've honored you with this choice. You are the first to join my coven in nearly five-hundred years," the goddess told me.

Shocked, I looked from the Goddess to Epona's house. Epona's door opened slowly. She stepped into the doorway, her hair all a mess. She pulled a blanket tight around her and squinted outside.

"Cerridwen?" she called.

With the most subtle twist of her wrist, the Death Goddess recalled her raven. It was then that Epona spotted her. I heard her gasp as she took two steps toward us then she bowed deeply.

"She is for the ether," the Morrigu told Epona.

Thora emerged from the darkness and padded across the coven square to me. She stood beside me whimpering softly.

Epona said nothing. I could see she was shaking.

"Do you understand, horsewoman?" the Morrigu asked Epona.

"Yes, My Lady," Epona answered hesitantly.

The Morrigu laughed. "You'll get what's yours. I've already agreed to that bit, but for now, it's time to play," she said then turned to me. "Before this one complicates matters further with her...will." With a flourish of her staff, the space around Thora and me began roll with twisting black smoke. It snaked around us like it was alive.

"Cerridwen!" I heard Sid scream.

I turned to see Sid rushing from her house toward us, a look of shock and fear painted on her face.

The Morrigu stepped forward, grabbed me by my neck, and looked at me face-to-face. Her eyes we dark as a starless night, her skin pale, lips red. "Why Gruoch, you look confused," she said with a laugh then everything went black.

twenty-three

THE MORRIGU LET GO. I twirled like I was trapped in the middle of a windstorm. Around me was a whirlwind of black smoke. I felt dizzy as I twisted in the wind. My head throbbed like it was being squeezed, and my ears popped. Then, I hit the ground hard. I was lying on the ground under a flower arbor. Enormous, long purple flowers growing on vines twisted around the ancient stone column. Their smell was sweet, like mint, milkweed, and lilacs. I had only seen them once before. Madelaine had called the vine wisteria. The world around me was lit in hues of black, purple, and silver. I closed my eyes and inhaled the wisteria's perfume. My ears were ringing; my head felt heavy. I felt disoriented, but I also felt very angry. Slowly, I sat up and looked around.

The arbor opened to a courtyard surrounded by crumbling stone columns. The flagstones glimmered silver. Wisteria grew all over everything. The sky was black; only scant beams of moonlight managed to slip though. Outside the circle of the cracked and tumbling columns, I could make out the shapes of half-tumbled buildings. Stones littered the ground. I was in a ruin. And at the center of the courtyard, in an ancient and decayed temple, was a cauldron. Beside that cauldron stood the Wyrd Sisters. The Morrigu was gone.

I rose and walked toward the women. My blood was thundering through my veins. My nostrils flared in fury. "Where am I? How do I get back?" I demanded.

The older woman, who stood bent and leaning against a staff, half-grunted, half-laughed. "You're in the otherworld, girl. Where do you think?"

"Come, Cerridwen," the younger woman beckoned. "Drink and be at ease," she added, dipping a silver ladle into the cauldron and lifting it, offering it to me.

"I need to go back. Now. Tell me how to go back."

"Why?" the old woman answered me in a voice that was too loud and too abrupt. Her voice echoed throughout the space. I realized then that wherever I was, it was very…empty.

I opened my mouth to answer, but she interrupted me.

"You cannot defy the Dark Lady, unless you wish for death. Or maybe she would just punish you by condemning your druid. You are here because the Morrigu wants you here. Would you disobey the Goddess of Death?"

I stared hard at the old woman who stared equally hard back at me. Then, after a moment, she chuckled. "Stubborn girl. Still stubborn as ever. Drink, Cerridwen. Drink and learn. I am not your enemy. I'm just a bubble of the earth," she said with a laugh then turned and sat down on a bench nearby. I stared at her. She was an ancient thing, her long gray hair nearly sweeping the ground. Her face was deeply wrinkled, and her fingers gripping the staff were gnarled and boney. Exasperated, she sighed and looked expectantly at me. When I didn't move, she flourished her hand in irritation toward the younger woman who still held the ladle, waiting expectantly for me.

"Come, sister," the red-haired woman said. "We will not harm you. Drink so you may know," she said.

Hesitantly, I moved toward her, eyeing her carefully. This was the first time I'd ever seen either of them very clearly. Every time I'd encountered the Wyrds before they had always seemed so mysterious. Now, they both seemed common: an old woman and her middle-aged companion. The younger woman's auburn locks curled down over her shoulders, and her eyes were hazel, a mixture of soft blue and green. She was, perhaps, the same age as Madelaine, and she was very pretty.

"Drink, daughter of Boite," the ancient woman said, tapping her staff, "so we can get on with it!" she added.

The red-haired woman handed the ladle to me. I was surprised when the metal felt cold to the touch. A hot fire burned under the cauldron, that was certain, but the ladle and the liquid were cold. I lifted the ladle. The liquid within smelled strange; sweet and vile at once. I eyed the red-haired woman who smiled encouragingly at me. I drank. The liquid was as cold as water from a frozen stream. I felt its chill as the liquid slipped down to my belly. For a moment, I worried I had been poisoned. I swooned.

"Grab her," I heard the old woman call before I dropped into unconsciousness.

Images flashed before my eyes like I was dreaming. I saw the cauldron courtyard and the wisteria arbor as it had been many, many years ago. I saw the ruins basked in sunlight. The place had been alive. The place where the cauldron sat was the courtyard of a temple. Like a ghost, I stood watching the world moving around me while everyone else was unaware of me. Everywhere I looked I saw priestesses dressed in dark purple robes with black capes. They moved through the wisteria-covered buildings chanting, swinging incense, and carrying offering bowls, many of which were filled with blood. They left their offerings before a massive, white-stone statue of the goddess that sat further within the temple.

Then I moved with the speed of thought beyond the walls of the temple, which sat on a hill far above the city, into the streets below. The city bustled. The citizens passed by, their bodies tattooed with symbols of death: ravens, skulls, weapons, even monsters. This was a city that reveled in death. Red-robed priests, carrying staves topped with skulls, passed in and out of a smaller shrine at the bottom of the temple stairs. Warriors carrying heavy swords dressed in glimmering armor hurried up and down the streets.

But the streets were filled with common people too. Rugged, seafaring commoners hustled down the streets: fishermen on their way to sea, mothers chasing children, old men driving mule carts. The people looked...content. They did not fear the priests and priestesses of death who intermingled with them. They nodded in respect. This island belonged to the dark lady. This was the home of death. Here, the Dark Goddess had ruled.

The images around me began to spin and blur, and I felt that I had moved forward in time. When I stopped again, it was in a scene of cataclysm. The ground shook. Even in my vision, I could feel the earth trembling. My knees felt weak. The ground shook. The people fled past me, through me, around me. The ground shook, and the buildings collapsed. Fire ravaged the place, and in terror, the people of the island fled in red-sailed boats into the wine-dark sea. The buildings collapsed. Those who stayed…well, their bodies littered the streets.

And when it was done, just as she had done to me, the Goddess of Death wove a smoky cloak around her island and pulled it into the abyss. She snatched her land, shifting time and space, and moved it into the otherworld. Her city hidden, her acolytes dead or dispersed, she shuttered her world in darkness, leaving it inaccessible to common man.

The vision left me. Pain shot across my head. I felt like a bolt of lightning struck me. I could feel someone holding me.

"Welcome home," the old woman said. Then, I slept.

IT WAS A LONG TIME before I woke. I remember what Sid told me about how time moved in the otherworld; days in the otherworld could be weeks or months in the human realm. There was no way to know how much time had passed. I was lost to the world of man. Lost.

Everything I loved had been taken from me. My friends. My husband. Everything. The Morrigu had snatched me up just as my life was beginning. She seemed angry that I'd dare to choose my own path, but she never bothered me even once before. All my life she had left me in peace: why would she demand ownership of me now? Why? I didn't dare command answers from the Morrigu, but the Wyrds...surely they knew.

It was dark when I woke. I was lying on a bed covered in deep purple satin. The room was very small. The walls were made of the same crumbling gray stone I had seen outside. Wisteria snaked through the window, into the room, and across the wall. It filled the place with its sweet scent. A corridor led from my room to the open space outside. I danced my hands across my body. I had been redressed in a dark purple velvet gown. A black robe lay across the end of my bed. It was the same clothing the priestesses had worn in my vision.

Quietly, I padded out of my room. Outside I found the stone courtyard with the massive center cauldron. The women were not there. I crossed the courtyard and went under the flower arbor. It was dark, but there I found a path leading downward. As I traveled, I recalled the vision the cauldron's potion had given me. I remembered that the courtyard was at the back of the temple of the Dark Goddess, which sat above the town. If I followed the path downward, around the side of the massive temple, I would emerge into the old city.

The temple rose high above me, its walls higher than any castle I had ever seen. The pathway was covered in rubble and wisteria grew wildly down the walls. Finally, I came to the end of the trail. There, I found a wide, stone-paved city street; it was the street I had seen in my vision. True to my vision, the city was in ruins and was completely abandoned. It felt so...hollow. I scanned around. The city street was lined on both sides with shops that had collapsed or been burned black. I also spotted the smaller temple I had seen in my vision, the one where I had spotted the red-robed priests. Everything was in ruin and charred. But when I closed my eyes, I still remembered the streets as they had been: bright, filled with people, children, and dogs. Dogs. Thora!

"Thora," I called, suddenly afraid. She had been at my side when the Morrigu had snatched me from Epona's coven. Where was she? Had she been left behind? "Thora!" My voice echoed through the dead city.

After a few minutes, a bark echoed through the hollow space.

The sound had come from further within the city. I rushed down the street, dodging fallen stones and massive fissures when there ground had cracked open, hoping that Thora was unhurt. "Thora!"

She emerged from a side street and ran toward me. I knelt and ran my hand across her black coat; her tail wagged with joy. "Are you all right?" I asked her, half expecting her to answer me. Instead, she only licked my hand.

"Cerridwen?" a voice called. The younger woman was walking down the street carrying a lantern in front of her. I noticed then that the light burning in the lantern was purple. She was dressed exactly like me: in a purple robe with a black cloak. "There you are. I heard you calling for your dog. Please don't worry. We've taken good care of her," the woman said. Thora trotted over to her. "I've missed the companionship of animals," she said, rustling Thora's ear playfully. "Please...I'm Nimue," she introduced then smiled apologetically at me. "I know how she brought you here," Nimue said then, linking her arm in mine. "I think the Morrigu forgets we are human. Andraste and I saw it all through the eyes of the cauldron. I'm sorry it was so jarring. Please, let me take you to Andraste. There is much to be said."

Andraste. Andraste. Where had I heard that name before?

"It was the same for me when I first came. One moment I was walking along the coast back to the cave I shared with my master, the next moment I found myself here. From that moment on, I belonged to the coven of the Dark Goddess." Nimue sighed then continued. "I was angry at first. I loved my master. But, in time, I came to understand my role."

"Who was your master?"

Nimue smiled at me. "Merlin."

"That's not possible," I blurted out. Even if Merlin had been real, he would have lived nearly five-hundred years ago.

"Time does not move the same here. For me, it seems like yesterday. I will let Andraste explain. She has been here a *very* long time."

I looked up the street at the temple, which had been so clear in my visions. The path around the side of the temple did not give justice to its glory. At its front, great steps led upward to the domed building that sat high above the town. What had been two exquisite statues of ravens now stood battered and crumbled at the base of the stairs. The temple's main body was circular. Wisteria had nearly overtaken the walls. Rubble lay on the steps though a path had been cleared to the top.

Nimue and I walked up the long steps, Thora bounding ahead of us. I was awash in a hundred different emotions. But most of all, I was determined to go home. My heart ached for my love. I gazed down at my hand. I was surprised to see that the knife cut had healed, and a scar had sealed itself over the cut. I stopped and stared at it.

"What is it?" Nimue asked.

"I had…I had a cut here. It's gone."

Nimue took my hand and examined the scar. "Was it a bonding ceremony?"

Apparently the Wyrds didn't know *everything*. I nodded.

She ran her hand over the scar. "Your druid?"

"Yes."

"Time has passed in the real world. Now you know how much."

"Banquo will be looking for me."

"He is a druid. He will understand."

"He will not abandon me here. And I will not be left here to rot!" I said, feeling indignant.

Nimue smiled softly and let go of my hand. "I remember what it feels like to love," she said in something of a whisper then turned and led me up the stairs toward the shrine.

As I followed behind her, I felt sorry. The Wyrds had always seemed…menacing. But Nimue was nothing of the sort. She reminded me so much of Madelaine. And if her words were true, then five hundred years had passed since she had loved. My anger must have seemed trite to her. Five hundred years was a long time to nurse a broken heart.

"Nimue?" I called.

She stopped.

I rushed up the stairs to join her. I was surprised and saddened to see her cheeks wet with tears. "I'm sorry," I whispered.

She shook her head dismissively. "It's all right. I understand you. Come," she said, then led me into the temple.

We walked through the crumbling hall into the main shrine. Here, a massive statue of the Dark Goddess lay on the floor. Her nose and arm had been broken in the fall. I remembered the statue of the Goddess as it had been before the earthquake. It had been made from crystal drug from the sea and polished to shimmer with sparkling white light. At its base, offering platters and vases were heaped with flowers, blood, and bones.

"This is the eternal flame of the Morrigu," Nimue said then, motioning to a large chalice, nearly five feet in height that burned with flickering orange and blue flames. The room smelled strongly of lamp oil. Nimue then led me down a hallway in the back of the shrine.

"Here is your room," Nimue said, extending her hand toward a hall on the left, and then we emerged onto the cauldron courtyard where the older woman, Andraste, as Nimue had called her, rested on a stone bench.

Thora wagged her tail and went over to her.

"Well, Graymalkin, up to no good?" the old woman said to Thora, gently setting her hand on Thora's head. I stood in silence.

The older woman rose, leaning heavily against her cane, then came to look at me. To my surprise, she pulled herself upright so she could look me in the eye. Her face was lined, and those lines had lines. But she smiled softly, and her eyes, which seemed very gray, crinkled. "I'm Andraste," she said.

Where had I heard the name before?

"Oh, it rings in your memory, doesn't it? Your face rung in my memory too. Always the queen, are you? Come, Cerridwen, sit," she said, then led me back to the stone bench.

"Do you remember anything?" she asked.

I frowned, not sure I understood her question. "I remember this place through the images your cauldron gave me."

Andraste grinned. "But do you *remember* this place?"

She was talking about soul magic. "I…I'm not sure."

"Cerridwen, when you drank the potion of knowledge, what did you see?" Nimue asked.

"This place as it had been and its fall."

"This place was once the most beautiful and magical of all places. Our people were strong. My father would go off to battle on the Morrigu's red-sailed ships. I remember how my mother, dressed in black and purple, would stand by the ocean and let drops of blood fall into the water to protect him. We did not fear death. Death was a passage.

"We worshiped the Dark Goddess in each of her aspects: battle goddesses, death goddesses, and goddesses of magic. Yet our lady destroyed us much as she destroyed others. She shook the earth. The people fled. When it was over, the island was empty and cluttered with dead bodies. And I, a small child, had hid in a trunk. It was the goddess of this land, the same who plucked you from Epona's grasp, who opened the trunk and bade me crawl out.

"She told me, 'I have changed what had to be changed. Now you are the only one left. You will age and grow old as one grows old in the otherworld. I will give you the ability to look into the world of man, and I shall council you on what must be done. You will do my bidding.'

"And I, a child of ten, became mistress of this island. And while I was a child, the Morrigu taught me what I should know. And now, I will teach you."

"But what is your...our...purpose?" I asked.

"We are the Wyrds. And now, finally, we are three. Now we will change the course of history."

twenty-four

LATER, AND I AM NOT sure if it was day or night since the sun never rose, Nimue took me to explore the city, Thora trotting along beside us.

"Why only darkness?" I asked Nimue.

"When she drew this island into the abyss, the dark lady cast out the sun. She permitted only her colors to rule in this place."

I looked around then said, "Black, gray, silver, purple, and red."

"White as well. All colors of the Dark Goddess. Silver is the color of the spirit of this world and of the Crone. Black and gray are the colors of magic. Purple is the color of the soul. Red is the color of war. White has many meanings; it is the color of divination, visions, anything involving power and consciousness. This is why the moon is sacred to all aspects of the Goddess. Its light is all-powerful."

It seemed to me that the Morrigu was like a petty child. She was capricious, killing and taking what she believed to be hers. When she'd grown weary of her people, she'd simply snapped her city into the otherworld, painted it with her colors, then went to play somewhere else. While I had no love for the White Christ, his priests—other than Father Edwin— sometimes counseled love and justice. Their Savior was said to have been a kind man. The Morrigu, on the other hand, seemed vicious.

But as much as I loathed her viciousness, I felt her within me. I knew she was right; I had belonged to her all along. I had been hers the night I took on my raven wings and killed Alister. I had always been hers, whether I knew it or not.

"Here we are," Nimue said as we stood outside the smaller temple at the base of the main temple stairs.

I looked up at the face of the building. Stone skeletal figures had been carved all over the walls. They fought with swords and carried shields. Whole legions of the undead were depicted fighting the living. Similar images existed throughout the city. Stone skeletons seemed to be a common decorative fixture.

"The priests were much like the druids of my time," Nimue continued. "They were acolytes, and bards, and warriors. They had an understanding of music and the power of resonance. Sound, they discovered, was a fabulous killer," Nimue told me as she pushed open the door. "But unlike my people, and yours, they also knew necromancy," she added, glancing back at me.

A shiver went down my spine. Necromancy. Just beside the door was one of the stone skeletons. Carefully, I reached out to touch it. It had a stain of blood on its head.

Nimue slapped my hand away. "Careful. This place is not quite as dead as it seems."

I stared into the empty eye sockets of the statue and got the eerie feeling that it was looking at me. I could feel its…disappointment. "Is it…what is it?"

"Sleeping," Nimue said. "You've heard the stories, I am sure, of how the standing stones that dot our beloved isle were once giants dancing with ladies. The truth of that story is not far off. You are looking at a hint."

I looked from Nimue to the skeleton and back to Nimue again. "Come on," she said, leading me within. "I'll explain later."

We stepped over broken stones as we made our way inside. The left side of the building was completely burnt. Nimue led us down a hall on the right and into a large room. The front of the room near the widows had a raised stone platform. Stone benches, most of which had fallen over, faced the platform.

"This is where they used to perform music. See how the wall is open there?" she asked, pointing to the far right. "The townspeople, though not permitted to enter the temple, were allowed to come to the courtyard to hear the priests play and sing."

Carefully, Nimue led me up some crumbling stone stairs to the second floor where we found the priest's chambers. Some of the bedrooms contained elaborately carved furniture that had begun to decay.

"You can't reach the third floor anymore," Nimue told me. "The stairwell was destroyed, but you can just spy the space from here," she said, pointing to a hole in the ceiling.

I gazed upward to see an overturned trunk. Plaster and stone loosened from the third floor ceiling and dropped to the floor overhead. It stirred up a swirl of ash, making both me and Nimue cough.

"We'd better go. The building is not stable." Nimue said, turning quickly.

As I turned to join her, I spotted something on the floor overhead. It was sitting just at the edge of the hole in the second floor ceiling.

"Wait," I said. "There, do you see that?" I asked her. I took a few steps to the side to get a better look. There, at the very edge of the hole, was a small silver box. "A box."

"Probably just an old stone, part of the wall or ceiling."

"No, no. It's silver. It glows. There, do you see it?" I asked, pointing.

She stood beside me and looked up. "It *is* a box."

I spotted a bench toward the side of the room, just tall enough to help me reach the hole in the ceiling. The temple groaned in protest as I slid the bench across the floor. From below, I heard stones clatter to the ground.

"Easy," Nimue cautioned, her eyes darting about nervously.

Nimue steadied the bench as I crawled up. I had to stand on my toes to reach the very corner of the box with the tips of my fingers. But working slowly, I was able to scoot it to the edge. It tumbled into my waiting arms. I crawled down and set the box on the bench. Nimue stood beside me as I opened the lid.

Inside was a pair of silver wrist torcs capped with raven's heads and a matching raven amulet. The ravens held glimmering purple stones in their beaks. Their eyes had been crafted with the same sparkling purple gems. The amulet was adorned with three silver ravens twisting around a large purple stone. The stone glowed. I had never seen anything like it before. The jewels were tarnished but in no other way damaged.

"Beautiful," Nimue whispered. "You must show these to Andraste."

I stared at the jewels. They were finer than any piece of jewel-work I had ever seen before. The silver looked very heavy, and the stones, well, I didn't know what they were, but they looked like amethyst. "It seems so strange to find something so old. So...lost."

"Just like us," Nimue said, then set her hand on my shoulder.

I looked up at her. "Isn't there a way out of here...a way back? Did you ever try?"

Nimue stared off into the distance. "Once. But I was...brought back. And not without consequences."

I closed my eyes and clenched my teeth. Anger seethed in me, and for a brief moment, I swore I heard my raven wings.

"Let's go," I said then, closing the box lid. I followed Nimue out of the temple.

As we headed back up the main stairs of the temple of the Dark Goddess, I remembered the skeleton statue that had stood outside the priests' temple. I turned and looked back toward the temple. My body trembled when I realized that the statue's head had turned; its dead eyes were watching me.

twenty-five

ANDRASTE WAS SITTING AT A table on the cauldron terrace. Before her was a basket full of fresh bread and rolls, their crusts flakey and golden, ripe red apples, grapes, and wheels of pale yellow cheese. She was drinking a huge goblet of wine. I stared at the food. I couldn't remember the last time I'd eaten.

"Well, curiosity sated?" she asked when we entered.

The bread's yeasty scent filled the air around me. Even from this distance, I could tell it was still warm.

"Cerridwen found a treasure," Nimue said.

When I didn't move nor speak, Andraste laughed. "Sit, child. Eat. You are hungry, aren't you? Didn't Sidhe tell you to remember to eat?"

"Where does the food come from?" I asked as I joined her.

Andraste handed me a hunk of bread, and I slid the box across the table to her.

Thora trotted over and sat down beside me.

Andraste laughed. "Here, Graymalkin," she said, then unwrapped a huge bone. It must have been lamb's leg. It was thick with meat. Thora struggled to get a hold of it, but eventually found a grip. She trotted over to the fire where she lay down and began chewing her prize. "It comes from the market, of course," Andraste finally answered me.

"What market?" The bread practically melted in my mouth. Nimue handed me a slice of cheese and a glass of red wine that I ate and drank greedily.

"Any market. I bought these in Glasgow."

I set the bread down. "Glasgow?"

Andraste opened the box. She stopped chewing as she stared at the jewels. "Where did you find these?"

"How did you leave?"

"In the priest's temple. Cerridwen spotted the box on the third floor," Nimue answered.

Andraste set down her food and lifted one of the torcs. "Beautiful. No doubt they were a hero's prize. Now they are yours. A gift from the goddess," she said, then slid the box back across the table to me.

"Certainly, our lady owed her a gift," Nimue said leadingly.

Andraste frowned at Nimue. She wiped her hands on a cloth napkin then looked at me. "Our lady is growing impatient and sloppy," she said, tossing the napkin onto the table.

"Don't let her hear you say so," Nimue warned.

Andraste puffed air through her lips in disgust. "Her charms are naught to me."

"She could curse you in the afterlife."

"Aren't I dead already?" Andraste answered with a laugh then turned to me. "What did you think of my city?"

"Strange."

"Indeed, it is strange. It's little more than a tomb now."

"Andraste, what happened to all the bodies? I don't mean to be insensitive, but..."

"But you felt them? They didn't go anywhere. And until you are ready, I suggest you don't creep far from the temple."

"The skeleton outside the priest's temple?" I asked, turning to Nimue.

"He refused to leave when the island shook, and he paid the ultimate price. Stubborn. Now he is like me, a relic," Andraste said with a laugh.

I suddenly felt very frustrated. "Andraste, why am I here? Why did she bring me here?"

"You are here to learn."

"As I did with Epona."

Andraste laughed. "Writing? Herb lore? Poems about trees? No, girl. You are here to learn what has been lost," Andraste said, then leaned toward me. "You are here to learn wizardry."

twenty-six

AFTER I ATE MY FILL, I went back to my small bedchamber to lie down. My head was turning over a thousand ideas at once: Banquo, the Morrigu, the black-haired man from my visions, Sid, the skeleton statue, Andraste, and…wizardry. Andraste said I would learn, not magic, but wizardry. The word itself was alive with power. I tried to sort it all out but it was useless. Before I knew it, I slept.

My sleep was fitful. In my dream, I walked down the street of the ancient city as it had once been. The priestesses in their purple gowns rushed up and down the temple steps. The red-cloaked priests wove amongst the citizens. They carried skull-capped staves and many wore head-dresses made of bone.

"Are you coming or not?" someone walking beside me asked. From the sound of the exasperation in their voice, I could tell it wasn't the first time I'd been asked.

I turned to find Sid, but not Sid, walking beside me. She had flowing black hair, dark eyes, and wore an elegant black gown made of silk and finely-spun lace. The gown was nothing like what the priestesses of the Dark Goddess or the common citizens wore.

"I'll come, but he won't believe me. No one does," I said.

Sid sighed heavily then reached out for my hand. I felt conflicted emotions swirl inside me, but then laced my fingers with hers. When I did so, I realized that I was wearing the purple robes of a priestess of the Dark Goddess. "*He* will," Sid said matter-of-factly.

Sid and I turned down an alley off the main city street. Here, the passage was narrow and dimly lit. The alley twisted and turned, and finally we came to the entrance of a small, slopping building.

"Stay close," Sid whispered.

We passed through the entryway into the low building. On both sides of the narrow entrance braziers burned with blue fire. Inside, skulls and bones lined the sloping walls. It was a catacomb. We wound downward, deeper into the earth. At the end of the long hallway was a cave. An elaborately carved door sealed the cave entrance.

"Are you sure?" I whispered anxiously.

"My Lord is not as cruel as some make him out to be. And, he always liked you," she said with a wink. "Stand back." Sid slid her finger around a myriad of shapes on the door. A trail of blue light followed her fingertip, illuminating the strange runes she traced.

The door opened slowly. Inside, the room was very dark. The heavy smell of the thick white sage rolled out. Under the smoky scent of sage was the loamy perfume of earth and mud.

"Come on," Sid said, then went inside.

My heart pounded in my chest as I followed Sid. I chewed my lip nervously. Inside, the cave was very dimly lit by the strange blue light. People dressed in black, just like Sid, moved in the shadows. The place was much larger than I imagined it would be; the ceiling of the cave was very high. There must have been more than two dozen tunnels stemming off from the main area, and wooden ladders led to cave openings on the upper levels. The place felt damp. A bat shrieked, and I could hear the sound of water trickling down the cave walls. The natural cave floor was wet. In the center of the room I spotted a tall throne. I looked away. Every hair on my body felt like it had been shot through with lightening. I shuddered.

Sid led us to the throne then stopped. "My Lord of the Hollow Hills," she whispered as she kneeled, pulling me down with her. I saw, for just a moment, someone seated on a throne before us, but he was hidden by shadows. I altered my gaze away from him.

He shifted in his seat and then, in a voice rich as velvet, he said to Sid, "Little Dia, why have you brought me an acolyte of the raven?"

"She is an oracle, My Lord. She's had a vision," Sid answered.

"Look at me, daughter of ravens. What have you seen?" he asked me. His voice was dark and sultry. Mesmerizing. I could not help but do what he asked. I looked up. Seated on the throne, leaning forward to look closely at me, was my raven-haired man. "What have you seen?"

"The end. We are doomed."

He leaned back against his throne. "We are like candles. Out, out brief candle," he said with a hard laugh.

I stared at him, but then the dream started to twist. I heard someone calling my name. At first the sound was very distant. I clung to the dream.

"I told you he would believe you," Sid whispered to me.

I looked once more at my dark-haired man, light and dark hues playing on his face. His pale skin was illuminated by the blue light. He looked exactly the same as I had seen him in my cauldron. He smiled at me, but I couldn't read the meaning of his expression. The smile was seductive and condescending all at once. I felt confused and a little afraid.

"Cerridwen?" someone called again. This time the call woke me from my dream. The sound echoed through the empty space.

Now fully awake, I sat up. "Hello? Nimue? Andraste?" There was no answer. I rose and went to the courtyard.

"Cerridwen! Where are you?" I heard someone call once more. It was not Andraste or Nimue. The voice was male. Banquo!

"Here," I whispered. "Banquo? I'm here!" I yelled, looking around.

"Cerridwen!" Banquo's voice rang through the hollow expanse. He was somewhere outside the temple, in the city itself.

Picking up my skirts, I rushed through the temple, passing the broken statue of the goddess, and down the main stairs.

"Banquo!" I called into the empty space. I looked everywhere for signs of movement. My eyes scanned past the priest's temple and I halted. The skeleton statue was gone. My heart skipped a beat.

"Cerridwen!" I heard Banquo call again.

I knew where his voice was calling from. I ran down the street and into the alley, retracing the same walk I'd made with Sid in my dream. Caves were hollow spaces where all worlds existed at once. Ruled by the little people of the hollow hills, creatures of legend, goblins or half-humans, such spaces were dangerous. But such places were also powerful passageways that could lead you anywhere. I ran to the outer door of catacomb. The blue lights still burned at the entrance.

"Banquo?" I called into the dark space below. My voice echoed.

"Cerridwen? Cerridwen, I heard you!" Banquo called back.

He could be anywhere. The hollow spaces were doors between realms, time. But then I remembered, Banquo knew how to walk between these realms. We had journeyed between the worlds on the night we wed. This was why he wore the marks of heavy earth magic; he had mastered realm walking. Banquo was a high priest of the Horned God.

"I'm coming!" I called to him. "I'm coming," I whispered, reassuring myself.

I walked into the dark cave. It had been damaged by the earthquake. Many of the skulls had fallen out of the wall and lay tumbled on the floor. I stepped on a leg bone that shattered under my foot, turning to dust. I coughed heavily when the heavy powder assailed my nose.

"My wife! Where are you?" I heard Banquo call.

"In a cave. I'm coming," I shouted back.

At the end of the hall, I saw a flicker of orange firelight.

"Banquo? Is that you?"

"Cerridwen?" he yelled. At the end of the hall where the catacomb met the cave, only one small blue fire burned. The doors to the Lord of the Hollow Hills throne room were open. The torchlight I had seen must have come from inside.

I moved carefully around the fallen stones and bones into the cave room. The sound of dripping water still filled the place. I cursed myself for not bringing a torch. Only one of the blue fires still burned leaving much of the place in shadow. The place felt wet and had the heavy scent of mud and algae mingled with a tangy smell of lime.

"Banquo?" I whispered as I scanned the tunnels. I saw torchlight flicker inside one of the tunnels at the far end of the cave room.

I moved toward it, but nearly stumbled on something. I looked down to see a skeleton lying at my feet. And then, as I scanned the room. Skeletons were lying everywhere. Then, I heard whispers. Someone or something was inside the cave.

"Cerridwen!" Banquo called, and this time I could feel he was close. I could see his torchlight moving along the walls of the tunnel. I stepped around a skeleton and headed toward the tunnel. I could clearly make out the firelight bouncing off the cave wall, coming in my direction.

"Banquo," I whispered and moved quickly, but suddenly, someone grabbed my arm.

I looked behind me. My heart skipped a beat. The skeleton from outside the priest's hall held me. His boney fingers dug into my flesh. He tilted his head then leaned in closer to me. Terrified, I couldn't move or breathe. The skeleton reached out his other hand and grabbed for my throat.

"Cerridwen!" I heard Banquo scream in terror.

I turned my head away to see Banquo standing at the entrance of one of the tunnels. A look of fear washed over him. The skeleton grabbed me by the back of the neck. Its boney fingers choked the air from me. I couldn't breathe.

"Cerridwen!" Banquo cried, and a second later, I heard a loud crack.

Forcing my head around, I saw the silhouette of Andraste. The crack I heard was her tall staff slamming hard against the floor.

"Go!" Andraste yelled at Banquo, her voice echoing powerfully throughout the cave. With a wave of her hand, black smoke enveloped the tunnel where Banquo stood, snuffing out his torch.

"No," Banquo shouted. His light faded.

"Banquo," I choked out, reaching for him, but he was gone.

"How now you secret, black, and midnight fiend?" Andraste growled at the skeleton. "Sleep, you stubborn fool," she added and then, tracing her finger in the air, she drew a strange rune. Blue light followed her finger. "Sleep," she commanded again.

The skeleton's hand loosened its grip, and the bones crashed to the ground with a strange hollow-sounding chime.

I coughed loudly the moment the boney fingers left my throat. "Banquo," I cried again and rushed to the tunnel where I'd seen him. The black smoke was gone, and so was Banquo.

"I told you not to wander," Andraste said.

"Where did he go?" I demanded.

"Home, I'd guess. Talented, your druid. No one has found this place in hundreds of years. But then again, he knows the shadowlands. Light," Andraste called then traced another rune in the darkness. Once again, blue light followed her finger. "Light," she called again after the shape was made.

At once, the cave sprang to life. Blue fires lit the square sconces all around the circular space. I finally saw the room clearly. It was filled with skeletons. And the man from my dream, the Lord of the Hollow Hills, still sat on his throne. His body had decayed to nothing more than bones, tatters of cloth hanging from his frame.

Andraste bowed to him then turned to me. "Come, girl," she said, beckoning me to her. "Give me your hand."

I did as she told me.

"Raise only your index finger," she told me. Then, taking my finger, she traced a rune with my finger on the palm of her hand again and again. "Now," Andraste said, letting go of me, "point your finger to the heavens."

I did as she directed.

"Select one," she said, motioning to the skeletons lying on the floor. "But not him. Stubborn fool. You are dead," she said, referring to the skeleton from the priest's temple. "And not him," she added, motioning to the Lord of the Hollow Hills.

"That one," I said, eyeing a skeleton that lay at the feet of the dead lord.

"Of course you would select her," Andraste said, then laughed. "Point to the heavens. Tell her, 'wake.' Make the rune then command her 'wake' again."

I knew what Andraste was teaching me…wizardry …necromancy. My body shook. I lifted my finger to the heavens, and this time, I felt power rush into my fingertip. It was like a bolt of lightning was racing into my finger and through my body. I shivered. "Wake," I told the skeleton. I made the rune in the air. The same blue glow followed my finger. "Wake," I said again.

The skeleton rose.

Andraste grinned as she took in the scene.

The skeleton's bones clattered as she shifted. Dust swirled around her. She took two steps toward me. Then the undead thing reached out for my hand. I was struck by the memory of my dream.

"Now what?" I asked Andraste.

"Now she is yours to command. She will do anything you ask."

I stared at the skeleton. Its dark eyes looked expectantly at me, its hand still outstretched. I shuddered. "I want it to go back to sleep."

Andraste took my hand. Again, she drew a rune in her palm over and over again. "Speak the word. Make the rune. Speak the word again then release the power back into the ground by pointing your finger downward."

"Sleep," I told the skeleton. Then I made the rune Andraste had showed me. "Sleep," I said again, then pointed my finger down.

The skeleton fell to the ground with a rattling crash. She lay on the ground before me, inanimate, though her arm lay outstretched, reaching for my hand.

twenty-seven

I SPENT THE NEXT SEVERAL DAYS working with Andraste, who taught me more of the mysteries of the Dark Goddess. One of the most important subjects Andraste taught me was history.

"This place is just one of many of the islands that exist in the otherworld. Surely you have heard the names of Atlantis, Lyonesse, Hy Brasil, and even Avalon."

It was then that Nimue, who had been sewing a hole in her cloak, looked up. She stared into the distance; her gaze was far away.

"You were a priestess of Avalon," I stated more than asked.

Nimue turned and looked at me. Her eyes were watery. "Yes," she whispered then went back to her sewing. She said nothing else. One day, I would be like her, forever mourning a life I'd missed hundreds of year ago. By the time I understood the Dark Goddess' magic well enough to master it, Banquo would be long dead.

And it was clear now, neither Andraste, nor the island, would let him come to me here. But then again, if what Andraste was saying about the other islands was true, then maybe there was still hope...still, a chance.

"Are there others, like us, on the other islands in the mist?" I asked.

Nimue raised her head and stared at Andraste.

Andraste smiled. "That's a good question. Perhaps."

"Could we reach them?"

Andraste shrugged.

"You haven't tried?"

Andraste shook her head. "I never had a reason."

I looked at Nimue. Excitement flashed across her eyes. In her, I knew I had a partner.

THAT NIGHT, I COULDN'T SLEEP. I kept thinking about necromancy, and dreams, and my feelings about Sid, Banquo, and the dark-haired man. The more I worried about getting back to Banquo, the more I missed Sid, the more I puzzled over the dark-haired man, the crazier I felt. It was like I had a whirlwind in my head. I wanted to learn the things Andraste was teaching me, but I also wanted to go home. I felt conflicted. Annoyed with myself, I got up. While I knew I shouldn't walk through the city, I also knew I could handle any skeletons that might come my way, thanks to Andraste.

"Come on, Thora," I said, stealing quietly out of the temple. I stopped at the top of the temple stairs and looked the city over. It was tragically beautiful: dark, covered in wisteria, fire-scarred. I hated being brought here against my will. Hated it. But there was something about the place that I had come to love. If the dreams and visions were true, I had been here before...with Sid and the dark-haired man at the very least. As Boudicca's memories lived in me, my memories of this place were starting to come back to me.

I headed down the main city street toward the docks. Nothing was moving. The skeleton was not back at the priest's temple. I hoped that meant he was still sleeping in the Lord of the Hollow Hill's throne room. As I neared the docks, I saw evidence that this really had been a nautical society. There was an open square where ships sat mid-construction. Several of them had fallen and were smashed, some burned, but they were still there. Heaps of wooden fishing traps littered the ground. What was missing, however, was the smell of the ocean and the call of sea birds. There was no roar of waves. I spotted the piers. Then, I saw the sea.

Three ships sat on an ocean of black smoke. Piers, at least thirty of them, jutted out into blackness. It was then that I really sensed the size of the fleet that had been lost. The ghost ships, their red sails hanging slack, sat in a sea of nothingness. Fearless, Thora ran up the steps and onto the main pier. I followed behind her.

The first ship I came across looked, up close, much like a Viking ship. The masthead was ornately carved. It was made of tan wood, and true to my visions, the sail was crimson in color. Age had dampened the brightness of the sail's hue. I jumped when Thora barked at the empty vessel.

I followed her gaze. The ship was moving. It pitched as if it were sitting in water, bouncing up and down as if small waves moved it. I looked over the side of the pier. The bottom of the ship was not visible. It was covered in black, and the blackness stirred, making swirling designs. The sea was still alive. And if it was still alive, that meant I could sail to the other isles.

Lifting a plank, I set it on bulwark. Thora jumped on the plank and bounded into the boat. Her feet on the rail, she looked out at me.

I laughed. "Okay, I'm coming," I told her. More careful than my dog, I shuffled up the plank and lowered myself into the boat.

I was surrounded by things I didn't know what to do with. There were pulleys, ropes, and other devices I couldn't name. I walked the length of the boat; it seemed sturdy. I entered the small captain's quarters. On the table was a map; its edges were yellow and crumbling. Thereon I saw other islands and the tip of the mainland. Some of the islands had names, but not the island of the Dark Goddess. I sat down in a chair and closed my eyes. A name. I needed to know the name of this place. I lay my hand on the map. It spoke to me in an ancient and dead language but one I nearly understood. Everything around me felt hollow. I felt like I was surrounded by cobwebs. The map below my hand began to feel hot. I started sweating. Through my mind's eye, I looked at the map. It was glowing with a red light. Names began to burn onto the map: Hy Brasil, Atlantis, Lyonesse… and then I saw it, the name I had been searching for: Ynis Verleath.

I was shocked. Yes, that was the name. I knew it. I remembered it. Ynis Verleath. I bounded out of the captain's cabin, off the ship, and down the pier. I rushed back to the temple. When I got to the steps, I shouted, "Andraste! Ynis Verleath!"

A few moments later, Andraste and Nimue emerged at the top of the stairs. "I remember! Ynis Verleath," I called to her.

"Come, Cerridwen," Andraste bade me. She had a serious look on her face.

Nimue looked pale and worried.

"Come," she called again.

My stomach dropped. Something was wrong. I nodded and headed up the stairs, Thora walking beside me. Andraste turned and headed into the temple. Nimue waited for me at the top of the steps.

"What is it?" I whispered to her.

She shook her head but took my hand. Together, we walked past the broken goddess and the flame of the Morrigu toward the cauldron courtyard. I could hear Andraste speaking to someone in low tones.

"Cerridwen?" A voice called.

It was not Andraste who'd called my name. Thora barked excitedly, and dodging around Nimue, she raced ahead.

"Cerridwen?"

When we passed the arbor, I was shocked to see Sid standing there. A green light glowed on the far side of the courtyard. Sid must have cut a door. If she could do that, why hadn't she come before? I realized then that Sid look frightened.

"Sid?"

She smiled weakly at me. "Hello, Raven Beak."

"What is it? What's wrong?"

"Uh..." Sid began hesitantly, sounding uncertain. She passed a glance at Andraste. "Nothing is wrong, sister, but you must return. A bridal contract is confirmed for you. Madelaine is here with us. She will wait for your return, but you must come at once. Mind the time."

A bridal contract was confirmed! At last, Madelaine had secured my marriage to Banquo. I closed my eyes and sent out a silent prayer of thanks to the Mother Goddess. "But the Morrigu...I never thought she would let me go so soon."

"So soon?" Sid asked. "Oh, my dear, I know your pains," she said with a sympathetic smile but then added, "It was the Morrigu who sent me, plucking me up with her talons and dropping me in the otherworld." Sid looked at Andraste. "I wish your mistress did her own bidding."

Andraste shrugged then sat down. "She loves for her own ends. Now Cerridwen will do her work in the mortal world."

"Cerridwen, my door is fading. I have to go. Come at once," Sid said, then stepped back into the swirling green light behind her, disappearing.

Out of the corner of my eye I saw Andraste and Nimue exchange glances.

"I can go," I said astonished. I had learned so little, but it didn't matter. Finally, I could return to my love. "I can leave!"

"A pity. A desperate pity," Nimue said, her voice filled with disgust.

Andraste shot her a sharp look. "Come, Cerridwen."

Andraste and Nimue led me to my room where Nimue gently disrobed me then redressed me in the plain dress I had worn the day I arrived.

"I've washed it," Nimue told me.

"It will make no difference," Andraste mumbled as she shoved the silver box containing the raven torcs into a bag which she handed to me.

"No," Nimue said bitterly. "You're right."

I didn't understand their words. "Why not?"

Andraste grimaced oddly, casting a passing glance at Nimue. "There is thunder, lightning, and rain. Now, where is Graymalkin?"

"By the cauldron," Nimue replied.

We went back to the courtyard. Andraste came to stand before space where Sid had stood. Opening her arms wide, Andraste whispered secret words and a portal opened. Black smoke swirled in a spiraling oval. It made my hair blow all around me. From within, I swore I could smell the scent of earth and rain.

Nimue pulled me into an embrace, kissing me on the cheek. "When shall we three meet again?" she asked, turning to Andraste. Her eyes were welling with tears.

"When the hurly-burly's done. Now, the world of man calls," Andraste said, and taking my hand, she led me to the portal. "My girl, remember, what's fair is foul and foul is fair," she said with a sympathetic smile. Her expression both surprised and worried me. "Now on with you into the fog and filthy air."

I turned and looked into the portal. I was going home. The Morrigu had set me free. Taking a deep breath, I entered the portal. I felt a strange pull as I was swept back to my world. But in the split second before I left Ynis Verleath, I heard Andraste speak. Her voice was full of sorrow.

"Something wicked this way comes."

THANK YOU:

Dear Reader,

I hope you enjoyed *Highland Raven*. If so, please consider telling your friends or posting a short review. You'd be amazed how much a great review helps to bring visibility to a novel.

Keep in touch! I'll be sharing information about Books II and III of this saga with my mailing list. If you would like updates, information about new releases, free short stories, and other book goodies, please subscribe to my newsletter.

Again, many thanks.

Best,
Melanie

AUTHOR'S NOTE:

DID YOU KNOW THAT SHAKESPEARE'S play *Macbeth* is usually referred to as *The Scottish Play* because many believe the play is cursed? There are numerous superstitions surrounding Shakespeare's tragedy. Some say the witches' lines are a real spell, others say the Goddess Hecate cursed the play because of how she was depicted (which leads many productions to exclude her character and lines), and others believe, very simply, that the play is unlucky due to all the deaths, theater closings, and unfortunate events that have surrounded its production. If you are an actor in the play, you must never say Macbeth inside the theater. It curses you. But not to worry, if you make a mistake it can be mended. You can spin around three times (note the number) or leave the playhouse then reenter to get rid of the curse. Regardless, *Macbeth* is a tale with power lying just under the words. Many times, I felt like my version of *Macbeth* was jinxed. And even in the hours before this book reaches launch, things are still going wrong. Hecate, take it easy, sister.

Bringing *Highland Raven* (formerly titled *Lady Macbeth: Daughter of Ravens*) to light has been a labor of love. In 1997, when I was a student at Penn State, I took a Celtic history class with renowned scholar Dr. Benjamin Hudson. When he lectured about the *real* Macbeth, it poured water on the seed of an idea. This wasn't the first time I'd thought about writing a novel on Lady Macbeth. My high school English teacher and I once discussed my idea. Was the real Lady Macbeth misunderstood? Could she be presented more sympathetically? How might Lady Macbeth's changing times relate to Shakespeare's vision?

I started writing and researching this novel in 2000. I won't claim this novel is an exact historical retelling. The amount of historical information on Gruoch is limited, and scholars disagree about some aspects of her lineage. I've done my best researching and piecing information together, but also I didn't want to drown the story in unnecessary historical detail. This saga contains the important elements of Gruoch's real life in addition to my creative embellishments.

I finished writing the novel in the early 2000s and started querying agents. I got a lot of encouraging responses. One agent, however, told me they had a client who was working on a similar book and couldn't consider me. A few years later, the talented Susan Fraser King published *Lady Macbeth: A Novel*. At the time, I was totally crushed. King (as a diligent researcher should) even consulted my former professor for her research. I was done. The jinx got me. I stuck my novel in a drawer and forgot about it.

In 2005, I shared an excerpt from this novel in a writing workshop. It got a positive response. I started working on the novel again. I knew King's *Lady Macbeth* novel was different from mine. My novel was about love and magic. My novel was fantasy. I got back to work and worked, off and on, (even during a long stretch of writer's block...jinxed again!), over the years.

In 2012, I published my first novel, *The Harvesting*, a dark fantasy/zombie mashup. Publishing was a great experience, and Gruoch still held a special place in my heart. I decided it was time for her to come onstage. I spent a year revising *The Celtic Blood Series* (formerly *The Saga of Lady Macbeth*.) In earlier versions of this novel, I called Gruoch by the nickname Gru. Thanks to *Despicable Me* (which came out in the interim), Gru was never going to work. Jinxed. Gru became Corbie (though I still call her Gru in my head).

This novel is a bit different from my other works. *High-*

land Raven is the first flame in a slow burn leading to an inferno. I thought it was important for readers to see Gruoch from the beginning. Her early life, growing up rough and devoid of love save for Madelaine's, profoundly impacts the decisions she makes in this book (where she is a rash 16 year old) and later in the saga. Gruoch is someone who desperately wants to be loved. That need, sometimes unconscious, blinds her to many things. In some ways, she is an unreliable narrator. She doesn't really know herself very well. *Highland Raven* also shows Gruoch just beginning to access her power. In later books, readers will see her wrestle with the dark forces inside her. And, of course, we will see Macbeth very soon. I look forward to sharing the next two books in this series with you.

In the playhouse, there is another way to remove the Macbeth jinx. If you cite some lines from another Shakespeare play, the curse can be lifted. So, without further ado (or, perhaps, this is much ado about nothing), let me just say:

If we shadows have offended,
Think but this, and all is mended,
That you have but slumber'd here
While these visions did appear.
And this weak and idle theme,
No more yielding but a dream

—*William Shakespeare, A Midsummer Night's Dream,*
5.1.423-428

ADDENDUM TO THE AUTHOR'S NOTE:
Summer 2015

The jinx won't go away! As the first edition of this novel went to publication, several major things went wrong. There were issues with the ebook, the paperback, an early review, and someone close to me telling me I shouldn't publish the book. I'll have to go back and look, but I think I must had tried to launch during a Mercury retrograde. Many, many tears were shed. Regardless, I pressed on. My fans, may the Goddess Cerridwen bless them, embraced the book. Great! But the problem was, the book just stalled. In a market where *Outlander* (I am forever a fan girl of Diana Gabaldon!) is big, why would a Scottish novel sink out of sight? I spent the next several months watching sales, considering branding, and wondering why Gruoch couldn't get off the ground (despite the wings).

After some research, we discovered that the branding of the novel was all wrong. High school English forever ruins many people on Shakespeare, even people who like to read. So why was I trying to sell people more of what they didn't like? I ADORE the first cover for this book. The gifted artist who made the cover designed the image right down to the detail of Gruoch's eye color, just as I asked them to do. The problem? I'm an author, not a cover designer. The book didn't say Scotland. Of course no one would look at it.

So here were are with a new name, a new cover, and a new plan. Will it work? Hecate only knows. Thank you for reading!

ACKNOWLEDGEMENTS:

A debt of gratitude to:

My husband and family for their tireless support of my writing career.

Muhterem Boz Karsak for all the sigara börek.

Cat Carlson Amick and Becky Stephens for their help in shaping this novel.

Carrie Wells for answering panicked texts.

Courtney Nelson for her sharp eyes.

My street team, the Airship Stargazer Ground Crew, for all the posts, tweets, fashion advice, positive vibes, and friendship. Your help is much appreciated. Love you guys!

My B.I.C. group members for all of the positive encouragement.

Margo Bond Collins for saving me from the yellow wallpaper.

The many hands that have touched this manuscript over the years. Thank you.

The bloggers! I owe a huge debt of gratitude to all the book bloggers for their reviews, promotions, guest posts, and most of all, their time. Thank you for sharing your love of books.

ABOUT MELANIE:

Melanie Karsak is the author of the Amazon best-selling steampunk series *The Airship Racing Chronicles* (*Chasing the Star Garden* and *Chasing the Green Fairy*) and the award-winning horror/dark fantasy *Harvesting Series*. She grew up in rural northwestern Pennsylvania and earned a Master's degree in English from Gannon University. A steampunk connoisseur, white elephant collector, Shakespeare nerd, and zombie whisperer, the author currently lives in Florida with her husband and two children. She is an Instructor of English at Eastern Florida State College. Find Melanie on the web:

MELANIE ON FACEBOOK:
https://www.facebook.com/AuthorMelanieKarsak
MELANIE'S NEWSLETTER:
http://eepurl.com/OSPDH
MY PINTEREST BOARDS:
http://www.pinterest.com/melaniekarsak/
MELANIE'S BLOG:
http://melaniekarsak.blogspot.com/
FOLLOW MELANIE ON TWITTER:
https://twitter.com/MelanieKarsak
EMAIL:
karsakmelanie@gmail.com
I'M A GOODREADS AUTHOR:
http://www.goodreads.com/author/show/6539577.Mela
nie_Karsak

Made in the USA
San Bernardino, CA
27 February 2019